The Sentinel

with every good wish
from

Maryann x

Also by Maryann Benbow

A Meeting of Souls
Soldier Part 1
Meeting the Past: Part 2 of Soldier

The Sentinel

Maryann Benbow

First published 2022

Copyright © 2022 Maryann Benbow

Dedication

For my grandson Nathan,

the light of my life

Contents

1

Freya

Freya sipped her morning coffee as she gazed out of the living room window, holding the letter in her hand. After decades of poverty, scrabbling a living on the breadline, the letter promised her an end to the struggle. Yet she could not, she would not, let herself believe it only to have the promise snatched away. Everything seemed unreal. Her body went through the motions, while it seemed as if her head floated six feet above her shoulders, a separate entity looking on dispassionately

She gazed unseeing at the street outside, her thoughts drifting in no-man's land. Her ramshackle house stood at odds with the pristine dwellings of her neighbours. The demands of simply living day-to-day had long taken precedence over the upkeep and maintenance the house had needed for so long.

It had been a happy house once, a home to be proud of. The sudden death of her husband had ended that, as she discovered the enormity of the debts he had left behind, the house mortgaged to the hilt. There had been no time to mourn his loss. The onus was on her now to provide for their two children and maintain the roof over their heads. All her energies had been needed to negotiate with his debtors and secure enough work to honour the agreements. It had meant little money for anything other than the basic requirements of daily living. The one focus of her life had been to ensure the children continued to enjoy the safety and security of their home. By working every hour God sent, she had succeeded. Both of her children were now settled with children of their own.

Freya glanced once more at the letter. After decades of financial struggle, it promised more money than she knew what to do with. Enough to secure not only her own future, but that of her children and grandchildren also. She had won the Lottery, or so it said. It was probably a scam. She dropped the letter on the table.

She picked up her car keys. As if in a dream, with no plan of where she was going or why, she left the house, which stood on the quayside of Whitby, and drove into the watery sunlight of the cold March morning. Two and half hours later, with the fuel and oil lights flashing a warning on the dashboard, she pulled into a roadside garage with a sign proclaiming its proprietors to be Olde and Bucket. The name badge worn by the red-haired attendant read "Rusty". Freya would normally have found the name tags amusing, but today they didn't register. In something of a monotone, she simply told Rusty what was required and sat back while he did his job.

"Have you driven far? The tank was almost empty, and the oil wasn't much better. All sorted now though." Rusty was poking his head through the open front window next to her as he spoke. His oily face sported an infectious smile.

"Not too far," Freya responded shortly. She paid him, thanking him in the same flat voice, which left Rusty in no doubt that his usual cheerful banter was not to be reciprocated.

The truth was Freya had no idea how far she had driven or where she was. As she turned left, back on to the road, she glanced in her mirror. Rusty was standing looking on as she drove away. Overhead, the trees formed a cool, shady canopy, casting a dense shadow on the road ahead.

She drove on. The road was unbroken for what seemed an eternity, but at last the car emerged from beneath the dark canopy into bright daylight. Up ahead the road forked and wooden signposts gave directions. The road to the left led to Masham; straight ahead led to what Freya hoped was a roadside pub: "The Sign of the Two Wolves". She needed a comfort stop, so continued onwards. At least now she knew where she was, having visited Masham and the surrounding area of the Yorkshire Dales many times in the past. It had, however, been many years since her last visit, and she had never heard of "The Sign of the Two Wolves". She imagined an ancient, almost forgotten, roadside coaching inn, but as she pulled into the crowded car park ten minutes later, it was clear she couldn't have been more wrong.

"The Sign of the Two Wolves" was a large, modern, stone-constructed bar and diner, built on the edge of a new estate. The sign in question took up a large central portion of the building and depicted a somewhat muddled image showing the sun and moon, horses, chariots and strange figures. The two titular wolves followed each other, leading all the other characters in what appeared to be a

10

circular dance. Freya paid the sign little attention as she entered the establishment, too intent on finding a loo. The smell of food made her realise how hungry she was, having left her home without breakfast. Feeling more comfortable as she returned from the ladies, she found a table and ordered an all-day breakfast and a latte. The breakfast, though it served its purpose, was as unremarkable as the establishment, and Freya didn't linger.

2

The Sentinel

Leaving the "Two Wolves" behind, Freya continued along the road through the new estate, following the bend to the right. It was then, as she crested a hill, that she saw it. A few hundred yards ahead and standing on a small hillock in a barren field, the ancient oak dominated the landscape, standing proud, commanding, and powerful. It seemed to call to her.

Freya was not a tree-hugger, but her first sight of this tree made her heartbeat faster and her stomach churn with excitement. She had no idea why, but she felt a jolt of recognition. She had to stop to have a closer look. A passing place close by offered a convenient spot for her to stop the car, so she got out to walk the last few feet to the field where the tree stood.

Curiously, all around, the other fields thrived, with green grass and hedgerows, but the ancient oak stood alone on bare brown soil. Doubtless, the earth had been sucked dry by its thick, gnarled roots, which spread, snaking and twisting, along the ground, intermingling with the enormous lower boughs which had long given up any attempt to reach skyward. Too heavy to support their own weight, they now rested upon the ground. The tree's green canopy of fresh buds would form a cooling skirt, providing shade and shelter, once it came into full leaf. For now, the burgeoning buds only held the promise of what was to come. The girth of its trunk was colossal. This remnant of times long past spoke to Freya's soul like nothing ever had before and she gave the tree her heart, knowing how ridiculous that would sound to anyone else.

She was contemplating going through the gate to take a closer look when a sudden voice behind her forestalled her.

"Mrs Thompson, I presume? I'm David Reeves, the estate agent."

Startled, Freya swung round to see a suit-clad man in his mid-fifties, with a smiling face and dark hair, extending his hand towards her. She returned his handshake, saying as she did so,

"I'm pleased to meet you, but it's a case of mistaken identity, I'm afraid. I'm Freya Fraser. I only stopped to take a closer look at the tree. I've never seen such an ancient tree before, so full of character. Imagine the stories it could tell, if only it could talk."

He smiled.

"Ah. the Sentinel has that effect on many people. The local area is full of legends and myths about its history. Some believe it dates to the Viking period, but what the truth is no one really knows."

"It has a name! 'The Sentinel'. Wow! I hope it has a preservation order on it. That new town back there is likely to expand and want to buy up the land. Those developers don't care what they destroy."

Freya felt genuine concern as panic and anger rose in her breast at such a possibility. This fear wasn't entirely allayed by David's response.

"It is indeed a concern. But currently the Sentinel stands on privately owned land, which is attached to the cottage I am under instruction to sell." He waved his hand towards the opposite side of the road. "I had high hopes that the client I was scheduled to meet today could be the answer, but it looks like a no show."

Freya had been too focused on the Sentinel to notice anything else before, but now she looked where he pointed. She saw a neat cottage set back from the road. It had a porch and two bay windows, one above the other, and an open garage attached on the left-hand side. The front garden was mostly gravelled, though the harsh landscaping was softened by a semi-circle of evergreen shrubs. A tangle of bare branches belonging to a climbing rose crept up and over the porch and a sign on the gate read "Sentinel Cottage". There were no neighbouring cottages, just the rolling patchwork of the green fields of the Dales, beyond grey drystone walls.

Freya had always dreamed of just such a setting. Quickly she glanced from the cottage back to the Sentinel, directly opposite, thinking how special it would be to live in the cottage and have the Sentinel for a neighbour. Her glance, and the desire in her eyes, was not missed by David. Like all estate agents he was eager to secure a sale and wouldn't miss any opportunity to do so. He glanced at his watch.

"It looks like my client has stood me up. If you fancy looking round the cottage, I have time to show you. What do you say?"

"I would love to, thank you," Freya heard herself saying, as the image of the letter she had dropped on to the table at home flashed through her mind.

Even as they crunched over the gravel (Freya's pet hate), she found herself planning the changes she would make. The first would be extending the garden and laying a new pathway. She had watched enough episodes T.V property programmes to know that the more essential changes were needed, the larger would be the reduction in the asking price – or so she hoped.

"We'll enter through the garage," David said, leading the way. He was now in full estate agent mode, waving his arm around the expansive garage, "As you can see, plenty of space for two cars, and towards the back there is a fully fitted utility area with a kitchenette, washing machine and dryer."

There was also a very large dog crate, Freya noticed, but David didn't comment on this as he unlocked the internal door leading into the cottage. It led into a galley kitchen that hadn't been refitted since the 1950s. Two doors led off: one straight ahead, the other to the right. David barely stopped to take a breath.

"The kitchen is small but perfectly adequate. Though it could be extended easily enough, either into the garage or into the dining room. To the right there is a downstairs toilet and shower room, and this is the dining room through here," he led Freya through the indicated door straight ahead, "with patio doors leading to the rear garden and land."

As he fumbled with the lock on the patio doors, Freya had time to glance round. As the room was unfurnished, there was little to see other than the décor, which, she decided, needed some freshening up and TLC. The wallpaper looked like it had been hung sometime in the 1960s. She followed David outside, where the beauty of the open landscape and rolling dales enchanted her.

"Oh, wow!" she said. The two words seemed to be the only words she could utter. David looked around at her, smiling.

"Breath-taking, isn't it? The garden extends to the river, just at the end of the field here. Then across to the left are two paddocks of pasture, and finally a small area of woodland known as Lucky's

Grove. There's about five acres in all, and of course there is the field where the Sentinel stands."

"Oh, wow!" Freya repeated, gazing about her. The land attached to the cottage was more wild and rugged than the gentle dale beyond the river where sheep grazed contentedly.

David, astutely, followed her eye-line.

"The garden has been neglected for a while, and the pasture has gone to seed since it hasn't been grazed. But it wouldn't take much to bring it back into shape."

Freya shook her head. "No. I like the wildness of it. It's as though it's a place beyond time. Foolishly romantic, I know." She laughed, suddenly embarrassed.

They went back into the cottage to complete the viewing, passing through the dining room into the lounge, with its view of the Sentinel through the bay window. A door to the right of the bay led to a small hallway, with front porch to the left and the stairs leading upwards to the right.

Freya followed David up the stairs. She noted the tired décor, the beautiful views from the two back bedrooms and the tired but adequate bathroom, then stood before the bay window in the front, gazing out at the Sentinel. The décor didn't matter. What had sparked her impulsive journey and directed her path to this point didn't matter. Only the why mattered. She already knew the reason, it was because this was where she was meant to be.

Without turning around, and dreading the answer, she asked David, "What's the asking price?"

She closed her eyes, crossed her fingers and held her breath as she waited for his reply, and after all that, she didn't quite catch what he said. She turned to face him, ready for some hard negotiation.

"I'm sorry, David, I didn't quite hear you. I heard the seventy thousand part, but what number came before it? Was it one, two or …?"

"You didn't mishear me, Ms Fraser. The asking price for the right person is seventy thousand pounds. It would naturally be a lot higher for a developer or someone wanting a second home or rental potential. I'm instructed to ask the minimum for the right person. I think you qualify. You have a feel for the land and its preservation, or at least that's the impression you have given me."

15

"There must be a catch. I love the place, but I'm not stupid. Why is the owner really asking such a low price? Come to think of it, why isn't he living here himself? The place hasn't been occupied for some time. Is it haunted?"

David laughed and held his hands up, palms out.

"To my knowledge, it's not haunted. In fact, in all my years as an estate agent, I've never come across a house that was. The owner has been in a retirement home for some time. The cottage was to have been inherited by his son, but tragically, that will now never happen. He was killed recently while on active duty with the armed forces in Afghanistan. Also, the owner realises the property needs a great deal of money spent on it. His main concern is to ensure it goes to a sympathetic buyer who will love, preserve, and protect the property and land. He also has no desire to see any profit going to the government for his care. So, there you have it. That's his ulterior motive."

Freya felt mean-minded and embarrassed to have asked. She decided to lay her cards on the table.

"I love everything about it, and I'd like to make an offer. No quibbles with the asking price, but when I set out today, I had no intention of either buying a property or selling my own. Even putting my house on the market straight away, it could still take time to sell. Would the owner consider renting it to me until I get my finances in place?"

David pulled his phone from his inside pocket. "I'll give him a call and find out."

He wandered into the hallway and closed the door.

Freya waited anxiously for David to return. She gazed through the bay window at her reflection and wandered who the washed out, grey-haired woman was who gazed back. Her anxiety quickly turned to relief and delight when he re-entered the room, smiling broadly.

"I have to say I've never negotiated either a sale or rental like this, but I'm delighted to say he is happy to agree a temporary arrangement, providing you can make a legally binding commitment to purchase the property at the agreed asking price within six months. If you can do that, you can move in as soon as you like, rent free, pending completion. If you can't meet the deadline or decide to pull out before signing the contracts, you will be charged six months' rent, at five hundred pounds per month. How does that sound?"

"It sounds like an offer too good to be true," Freya laughed. "I accept."

"That's a start then. But there is another caveat that you may well need to think about. I mentioned the owner's son was killed in action. He had two military companions, of the four-legged variety, that he always intended to stay with him after he left the army. They are familiar with the house and territory. The owner requires them to have a home here, out of respect for his son's wishes, if you are willing to take them on. They are well trained and generally need little attention other than providing them with food, water and a place of safety. Exercise wise, they will roam free, within the property boundary, or accompany you on your walks. They will come to heel as soon as they hear their name. But it's understandable if you don't feel you can meet this request."

The smile left Freya's face and she chewed her lower lip.

"Oh, no! I knew it was too good to be true. I have to be honest, I'm not really an animal sort of person. Not that I would ever hurt one, but I don't go all gushy with longing when I see one."

David's phone pinged, as if on cue, and after glancing at it briefly he passed it to Freya. There was an image of a smiling young man in uniform, with two large dogs sitting in front him, looking attentively at his face. They looked like huskies, or maybe malamutes. Both wore military-style coats, bearing the regimental insignia. She gazed at the image intently, so many thoughts spinning in her head. David broke the growing silence.

"Privates Fen and Arty, but I have no idea which is which. They are being flown back to a military base in England. I can work with the owner and military to arrange for you to visit them if you'd like to before making your decision."

Freya hesitated, torn between making a commitment to care for two large dogs and losing the cottage that she already felt was her home. But then, it was their home too, wasn't it?

"Oh, what the heck! Let's do that. They may not like me either, but let's give it a go."

3

Fen and Arty

It was almost two weeks later when Freya found herself driving into an army training camp in Yorkshire and asking to be directed to the Canine Personnel Academy. The day was overcast, and April showers threatened.

As she got out of the car, she was glad to find David waiting for her. Passing through all the checkpoints guarded by soldiers with guns had been nerve-wracking. She had even been modestly searched at one point, as had the car. Despite their brief acquaintance, Freya was so relieved to see a friendly face that she almost flung herself into his arms. He, however, was the consummate professional.

"It's a pleasure to see you again, Ms Fraser. Thank you for coming. I apologise for the imposition by my client. To be honest, I find it a bit of an imposition myself. But we are here now. Shall we move things forward? I believe we must pass through that gate there."

He pointed towards yet another checkpoint just beyond the car park. This time it seemed they were expected. They were waved through, and a young cadet was given the task of escorting them into the Academy, where they were asked to take a seat.

"Captain Lockheart will be with you shortly," the cadet told them before marching smartly away.

Captain Lockheart was a tall, dark-haired man in his thirties, with an athletic physique and handsome features. Freya stood as he approached quickly, announcing his presence.

"Not such an imposition after all," she thought with feminine appreciation, age being no barrier to the delights of good eye-candy. "I wonder if he comes with the dogs?" But as she held out her hand for the formal introductions, she maintained a more decorous manner.

"Ms Fraser, it's my understanding you wish to be considered as the guardian of Private Fen and Private Arty. I have to say it's an unusual situation. The military does not normally hand trained personnel over to individual civilians. However, Major Winguard was a friend of mine. I know it was always his intention to retire with Fen and Arty to the family home. I understand his father, Colonel Winguard, is eager to see his son's wishes fulfilled, at least in part. Perhaps we could go to my office, go through their files, and discuss the best way to proceed."

Once Captain Lockheart had ensured their comfort and supplied tea and biscuits, he got down to business.

"I've spoken with Colonel Winguard at some length, so I'm fully aware of why you wish to take on the guardianship of Fen and Arty, Ms Fraser. But what do you know about them?"

Freya shook her head. "Absolutely nothing, to be honest, other than they are huskies, and I can't tell them apart. This meeting is to address that and to ensure that Fen, Arty and myself are equally happy to become a family unit. It has to work for all three of us."

Captain Lockheart looked up sharply as Freya mentioned huskies and shot David a piercing stare. David appeared oblivious to it as he tapped on his phone and handed it to Freya. It showed the image of the dogs he had shared with her previously. In turn she gave it to Captain Lockheart, though he barely glanced at it. Instead, he removed two photographs from the file and pushed them across the desk, one at a time.

"They are full brothers and are remarkably alike. Private Fen, as you can see, has the most striking amber eyes. Private Arty, on the second photograph, can be recognised by his extraordinary ice-blue eyes. But I would be failing in my duty to you, to the animals and to the army if I didn't tell you, Ms Fraser, that Fen and Arty are pure-bred wolves, not dogs of any breed."

David dropped his cup, spilling his tea everywhere.

Freya laughed nervously.

"This is an April Fool's joke, right?"

But she knew by the look on his face that Captain Lockheart was deadly serious. In her mind's eye, she saw the loss of the house she loved. There was no way she could take on the responsibility of two wolves. Could she? Yet if she didn't, what would become of them? The army clearly no longer had a place for them. The streets were full of ex-servicemen, discharged with no home and no care package for the injuries and trauma they had suffered while serving their country. Freya might be naïve, but she wasn't stupid. For Fen and Arty it would be a no-return trip to the vet.

She looked down at the photographs now clutched in her hand, then burst into tears. She was crying for herself, for Fen and Arty, and for all those tossed on the scrap heap once they had served their purpose. David offered her his handkerchief, then retracted it when he realised it was soggy and dripping from mopping up his spilt tea. Captain Lockheart, who could remain cool and calm in the heat of battle, had no idea how to deal with the tears of a woman. He attempted to escape.

"Forgive me, Ms Fraser. It was not my intention to cause you distress. I will give you a minute or two to collect yourself."

Freya caught his hand as he reached the door.

"Don't you dare go sneaking off to give orders for the destruction of those innocent boys."

He smiled. "Believe me, Ms Fraser, such a thing had not entered my head. I will be back shortly. Mr Reeves, a word outside if you please."

As the two men departed, she could hear the captain giving more orders.

"Sally, can you tend to Ms Fraser? A box of tissues and more tea if you will be so kind. Follow me, Mr Reeves."

Sally, (whose name tag declared she was officially Corporal Sarah Thorenson,) arrived with the required tissues just in time to save Freya from wiping her nose on the cuff of her jacket.

"Captain Lockheart thinks you may need tea and sympathy, but I think a visit to the washroom and some fresh air may be preferable?"

Freya summoned a weak smile, followed by a sniff.

"That would be wonderful. Thank you."

Twenty minutes later, Freya was back in Captain Lockheart's office, feeling refreshed and more confident after chatting to Sally. Much of what she heard from Captain Lockheart during the next hour, she had already learned unofficially from Sally. Neither Fen nor Arty had been trained to attack and both were trained for patrol duty, making use of their natural instincts to protect their territory and their pack. Only when either of these was threatened would they fight, not as aggressors but as defenders. At the time of Major Wingard's ambush, both Fen and Arty had attacked the enemy in his defence, showing their courage and loyalty, both natural traits. In doing so, Fen had sustained a stab wound to his shoulder. Arty had been grazed by a sniper's bullet. But they had pinned the attackers down until help arrived. They were heroes.

The other snippet of useful information was that wolves would kill only for food, if they were driven by hunger. If well fed, they would not be inclined to hunt local wildlife, farmstock or pets. The key to handling them was, she was assured, to establish her role as leader of the pack, and maintain it.

It all sounded very positive, but Freya knew it was easier said than done. Nevertheless, Captain Lockheart felt he had prepared her sufficiently to move forward. He began shuffling the file contents together, then leaned back in his chair.

"Well, Ms Fraser, I believe I have prepared you all I can. If you feel you would like to go forward and meet Fen and Arty, I will take you to meet Major Hodson. He will introduce you to them and discuss the way ahead. But remember, no one will blame you if you feel unable to take it further."

Freya sat up, straight-backed, then stole a look at David, who hadn't said a word since his private chat with Captain Lockheart. He continued to make no contribution. She took a deep breath, before saying,

"We've come this far, so taking the next step seems logical. But let me be clear. I am not making any commitment at this stage. It's just baby steps to see where it leads."

"Understood," Captain Lockheart replied, then bellowed for Sally. Entering the room within seconds, she received her orders.

"Let Major Hodson know we are on our way across to the parade ground, please, corporal."

No sooner had she left with a brisk salute, than Captain Lockheart was also leading Freya and David out of the room.

For the next hour they watched from a gallery through a Perspex screen at the arena below as what appeared to be a whole battalion of dogs (maybe wolves, Freya couldn't be sure) were put through their paces. It was fascinating to observe the obvious bond between animal and handler, and both Freya and David clapped enthusiastically when they left the arena, as though they had been watching an entertainment show at a country fair.

"Shut that damn racket up!" A voice bellowed over the speakers and Captain Lockheart looked embarrassed.

"Oh dear, I should have warned you. The major insists on total silence while the training sessions are taking place. That's even more important today as this was the final exam before they are admitted to active service."

"Damn right you should have given due warning, Lockheart. It would have saved me the trouble of bellowing to uneducated civilians. Damn pain in the neck!"

Judging by Captain Lockheart's swift jump to attention and his crisp salute, there was no doubting the man who now approached was Major Hodson, making the captain's somewhat embarrassed introduction superfluous. The major turned his attention to Freya.

"Ms Fraser, you look like a puff of wind would knock you over. What makes you think you could control a wolf?"

"I don't think anything of the sort, Major. That's what I'm here to decide, after I've met them and been given all the information I need to make an informed choice. Which is your responsibility, I believe."

Freya's response was barbed. The man hadn't made a good impression and she was seething. So was the major,

"Now look here, Ms Fraser. I'm a very busy man. I don't have time for you to be playing games and faffing about deciding if they match the colour of your eyes or your latest outfit. You do realise that you're playing with the lives of army personnel? Your decision is a matter of life or death. Do you understand?"

Freya didn't know whether to slap him or spit vitriol at him. Instead, she clenched her fists tightly until her fingernails dug into the palms of her hands, then counted silently to ten, taking a deep breath before speaking.

"I understand the situation perfectly, Major, so let me disabuse you of any misconceptions you may be under. My own future is also dependent on a positive outcome here, which is why I will do all I can to bring that about. I won't, however, put myself, my family or Fen and Arty in danger, so I will go ahead only if I am confident that I have been given the level of competency required to take on the care of the two wolves. That will be down to you, and I am in your hands. At this point in time, I don't even know if I have the competency to care for two Yorkshire terriers. Time will tell.

22

But I will not be bullied or emotionally blackmailed into making the wrong choice. God forbid that any decision will see those poor beasts served a death sentence. But if they are, it will be on your head, Major, not mine."

Freya was breathless, her chest heaving, by the time she had finished speaking, not just with the effort but with pent-up anger and emotion. Standing behind the major, Captain Lockheart dared to give her a wink and a thumbs up. David showed his support by taking a step forward and placing his hand on her shoulder.

"You have backbone, at least, Ms Fraser," the major said, before turning to the captain. "Dismissed, Captain. Return to your duties. I will assume responsibility for Ms Fraser."

Just in case the major tried to dismiss him also, David quickly established his position.

"I'm representing Colonel Winguard, Major. My instructions are to oversee the process and report back to him. So, I'll be tagging along."

The major gave a curt nod and led the way briskly to the training kennels. On their way, Freya was able to study the Major. Though far from being small, his stocky build and unhealthy paunch, gave him the appearance of being somewhat squat. He walked with a straight back and purposeful stride, exuding authority.

The kennels were both noisy and busy, and Freya felt her sense of anticipation mounting as the major led the way down a row of tall, spacious kennels, where the handlers were busy grooming their charges or cleaning the space. Dogs were being taken out for exercise, others were returning from their exercise. Not one of the men or women failed to acknowledge the major's presence with a sharp salute and a respectful "Sir", as he continued to lead Freya and David forward and through a door at the end.

The room was large. A small, comfortable reception area held a large desk, behind which an army officer was sitting. As they entered the room, he rose quickly to greet the major, snapping to a straight-backed attention and an instant salute. Freya barely focused on the introductions. All her attention was held by the large, floor-to-ceiling kennel which dominated the space. One wall of the kennel held what appeared to be a small garden shed, draped in a camouflage net. From this emerged the two wolves, whose behaviour held the key to Freya's future. There was no question of their identity. Fen's thick grey fur turned to a light shade of beige across his chest and down into his long legs, and his light amber eyes held her gaze. Beside him, his brother, Arty, whose fur, the palest of grey bordering on silver, blended into white across his chest and down into his legs. His eyes were the colour of a winter sunlight, blue, holding the touch of ice and Freya stared back, mesmerised. Involuntarily she took a step forward. Fen copied with a half-step towards her. Arty did not move, but he held his head higher and seemed to flex his shoulder muscles, suddenly looking taller and broader.

A sharp voice broke the spell.

"Ms Fraser! Face me instantly with your back to the kennel. Private Fen, stand down! Private Arty, at ease!"

There was an urgency in the commands which Freya could not ignore. She obeyed instantly, not waiting to see if Fen and Arty did the same.

It had been the desk sergeant, Sergeant Erickson, who had given the command. Now he made Freya the object of his attention.

"Lesson one, Ms Fraser. Never make direct eye contact with either a dog or a wolf. They see it as an aggressive challenge and will respond aggressively. Count yourself fortunate that the attack you have just instigated occurred in a controlled environment and was averted. Lesson two, these animals are not domesticated. They remain wild in every sense. We have been successful in utilising their natural behaviour, not by humanising them but by changing our own way of thinking. We've merged ourselves into the social system of a wolf pack and established ourselves in the hierarchy as pack leaders by building up a rapport and trust with other pack members. They have not been trained but merely socialised to recognise certain commands. Do you understand all this, Ms Fraser? Have you any questions?"

"No questions. I understand what you've told me and I'm so very sorry I screwed up."

Freya replied quietly, embarrassed, and heart-sick that she had just thrown away everything she had hoped for. She turned to David.

"David, I'm sorry to have put you to so much trouble for nothing. Will you also pass on my apologies to the colonel, please?" A single tear ran down her cheek.

Surprisingly, it was the major who offered her the comfort and assurance she needed to give her hope once more.

"Come now, Ms Fraser. All is not lost. Unless you wish to call it quits, and I didn't have you down as a quitter. Are you feeling ready to go on? Some bravery will be required, but I know you are not lacking there."

Freya was surprised not only by the major's encouraging words, but by his supportive actions also. She looked up at him.

"What do I need to do?"

Fifteen minutes later, armed with a cup of tea and a magazine, Freya sat on the step of the wolves' kennel, her back to them, with instructions not to acknowledge them in any way. Draped over one shoulder she wore Major Winguard's old army coat, the scent of which reassured the two wolves that their pack leader was close by and all was well. She had removed her own coat and sweater, having been told that her tee-shirt would hold her body odour much more strongly with the outer layers removed. How delightful, she had thought with some distaste, though she understood the purpose was for the wolves to get to know her scent and associate it with the man they had given their trust to. She was not invading their territory, but she was close enough for the wolves to investigate.

As she felt the warmth of their breath on her neck through the bars of the kennel, her hands shook, but she feigned nonchalance, lifting her cup and sipping the strong, bitter tea. The weight of a heavy paw pressed the chain-link fence (covering the bars for extra security) against Freya's shoulder and rested there, over Major Winguard's old coat, for a minute or two, before it was withdrawn with a small whimper. The gesture tugged at Freya's heart. She didn't know which of the wolves that paw belonged to, but she felt certain it was a gesture that tried to reach out to the man who had cared for them, perhaps trying to understand what had happened for him to withdraw that care?

Freya brushed tears from her eyes before they could run down her cheek. Putting the magazine aside and clutching the mug of tea in both hands, she began to speak quietly, almost to herself.

"Once upon a time there was a little girl called Freya. Sometimes, when the winter winds blew and the snow began to fall, she would wrap up warm in a red cloak, pulling the hood up to keep the chill at bay."

At the sound of the unfamiliar voice, both wolves became alert, pricking their ears and putting their heads on one side as though listening with extra care.

"One day, when the winter wind blew strong, Freya had to go on a journey to visit her grandmother. She knew of the dangers of travelling through the woods, but she knew something else too. There had once been a man who took care of the wolves. Keeping them safe and fetching them food when it was hard to find. The man had gone now. Something bad happened to him, so the wolves no longer had anybody to help them."

The men sitting around drinking their tea and keeping an unobtrusive watch on Freya and the wolves sat up in their seats. They exchanged surprised and puzzled looks among themselves, recognising the basis of the old fairy tale, "Little Red Riding Hood". But they kept silent as Freya went on.

"As the howl of a hungry wolf travelled forlornly on the freezing air, Freya made a silent promise to the wolves. She would do whatever she could to help care for them. When she got to her grandmother's house, she took three of her grandmother's chickens. One she killed and cooked for her grandmother's meal. The other two she put into a sack and released them later in the wood. If the chickens were lucky, they would find their way back home. If not, then at least one or two of the wolves would not go hungry. Freya had done all she could to help the wolves, and she always would."

Freya paused to sip her tea and looked across at the men, all smiling in approval at her. Major Hodson silently gave her an approving nod, then indicated that she could quietly leave her hard seat and re-join them. When she glanced around, she saw the wolves stretched on their sides, sleeping. She smiled.

"Have I hypnotised them or bored them?"

"Be proud of yourself, Ms Fraser. You have convinced them that you are not a threat, and that is a huge step to have achieved in one day."

Sergeant Erickson shook her hand. "I take my hat off to you, Ms Fraser. Your method may have been unconventional, but we have achieved all that was needed for today. You will need further, more formal training. If it's all right with you, I will telephone you with the arrangements."

Freya agreed and soon found herself heading towards her car, with David beside her. As they prepared to part company, David placed his hand on her shoulder.

"How are you feeling?" he asked, searching her face. "Really."

"Really? Elated, anxious, but above all totally exhausted," she responded.

He gave her a hug.

"Drive carefully, Ms Fraser. I'm going to tell the colonel you have complied with his request. Whatever happens, no one will do more. I'll be in touch in a day or two."

Overwhelmed, she had no words with which to thank him, but her smile and the light in her eyes said all that was needed. She gave him a wave and a toot of the horn as she drove away.

4

New Beginnings

Over the next six weeks Freya was busier than she had been in a long time. It began even before she had undertaken more training with Fen and Arty.

David had telephoned the next day to say the colonel had agreed to go forward with the sale, satisfied that she had done all she could to meet the terms agreed. Her lottery win had also been confirmed. Freya could not have been happier, or more excited.

Confident that a brighter future was assured, she wasted no more time in letting her children know the good news. They arranged to hold an impromptu housewarming that weekend, when she would sign all the paperwork and receive the keys from David. She gave them the address and told them to bring sleeping bags, warning them the house needed a lot of work before it could provide them with comfortable accommodation. But she was looking forward to showing them the house and roping them in to help her plan the renovations.

Her son, Daniel, arrived first, accompanied by his wife, Lisa, and their boys, Jack and Jamie, just as David was leaving. Amidst the kerfuffle of introductions and greetings, Freya's daughter, Marie, also turned up, with her two children. Rose was the eldest of Freya's grandchildren, Aston, the youngest.

In due course, Daniel took the boys to explore the grounds, to let them run off steam after the long car journey, while Freya led the girls on a tour of the house. There was no lack of enthusiastic suggestions for improvements and Freya was at her happiest and most carefree for a long time. They all loved the house as much as she did and agreed it was full of potential.

David returned for the evening housewarming, bringing with him a surprise guest, Captain Lockheart. Freya greeted him and whispered in his ear,

"For God's sake, don't mention wolves. My children will have me certified!"

He laughed. "My lips will remain sealed."

Both men made themselves at home, mingling with her family quite happily. Captain Lockheart and Marie seemed to hit it off straight away, spending most of the evening either deep in conversation or dancing with abandon. Freya watched, hopeful that her daughter, following the breakdown of her marriage, was also on the way to finding the fresh start she was looking for.

As the aroma of barbecued steaks drifted across the fields, accompanied by laughter, the clink of champagne glasses raised in toasts and music from every era from the 1950s to present day, only one cloud shadowed Freya's thoughts. The wolves. Would she prove worthy to be given responsibility for them, and how would her children react when she told them about her commitment?

Daniel and his family returned home the next day, but surprisingly Marie volunteered to stay to help plan and oversee the renovations. Since the house wasn't ready for long-term occupation, they booked into guest accommodation at "The Sign of the Two Wolves". After a day spent going from room to room in the cottage, making notes and researching contractors to submit quotes for the work, they all delighted in the luxury of a hot shower and a much-anticipated cooked meal at the diner. Over dinner it became apparent that Marie had a secondary motive for offering to stay.

"How do you know Peter, Mum?" she asked, trying to sound nonchalant.

"I don't know him," said Freya, reaching for her glass of wine. "Who's Peter?"

"Mum's got a date with him," Aston blurted out.

"Has she? I still don't know who he is, Marie."

"You do know him," Marie insisted. "He was at your party last night. He came with the estate agent."

A smile of enlightenment flashed across Freya's face,

"Oh! You mean Captain Lockheart! I didn't know his first name. He seems nice enough, but I've only met him once. He's in the army. Have you got a date with him?"

Even as she spoke, Freya surprised herself. She really had only met the captain once, yet it seemed their acquaintance had been longer.

"I have, as it happens. So how do you know him?"

Freya decided to come clean. Mostly, at least. She told them the full story of the conditions for the sale of the cottage, and how she had met the captain when she went to be introduced to Fen and

Arty. She avoided mentioning that they were wolves as she showed them the pictures on her phone.

They all thought they were beautiful animals, but all offered different opinions.

"Wow! When the snow comes, they can pull us along and take us for a sleigh ride!" Rose was delighted at the prospect.

"My god, Mother!" said Marie. "Beautiful as they are, you'll never be able to manage them. They'll be far too strong for you, and you've never owned a dog in your life."

Aston gazed at the image thoughtfully, before saying, almost in a whisper, "The tree wants them home. They are the wolves Fenyr and Haati, and they belong to the Sentinel."

For a second or two Freya was taken aback. Then she realised the menu of the "Two Wolves" had the legend of Fenyr and Haati printed on the back. The picture could well have been that of Fen and Arty. Could the names of the legendary wolves have been the inspiration for their names? She was proud that Aston had associated the names, and at how quickly his imagination had expanded the myth to include the Sentinel.

With the sudden arrival of Captain Lockheart, the opportunity to respond to Aston was lost. Marie, in a hurry to escape on her date, excused herself.

"I won't be late, Mum, I promise," she said as she kissed Freya on the cheek, confident that even though she hadn't asked, her mother would willingly take care of the children.

"Enjoy yourself," Freya said. "And no need to rush. We aren't going anywhere. Treat my girl with respect and take care of her, Captain, or the whole of the British Army won't be able to protect you."

"You have my word, Ms Fraser," he replied. "I wouldn't dream of treating her any other way."

As Freya's plans moved forward, so did Marie's, much to the delight of her mother. As she and Peter became established as a couple, and the renovations to the cottage were almost complete, Marie made the decision to accept Freya's offer of help to buy a house in the new town. It was close to both her mother and Peter, and gave her the chance for her fresh start. David handled the sale, and on the day that Marie signed the contract, Freya heard that she had formally been accepted as the custodian of Fen and Arty.

It had not been easy for Freya to reach this point. Her training had been intense, undertaken alongside a group of new recruits to the Academy, and no allowances had been made for her status as a civilian. After a week of attending lectures and watching endless videos, she had developed an understanding of the techniques and commands needed to control and reinforce the behaviour required of Fen and Arty. There followed a week of taking on the sole responsibility for their daily routine, their feeding, grooming, exercise, and training.

Establishing her role as pack leader had been the most demanding part. Day and night, she lived in the same kennel as the wolves, eating and sleeping alongside them. She took her breakfast first before offering the wolves their meal. Without using any physical barriers, she established that her sleeping and eating space was a no-go zone for both her charges. The daily routine expanded to include taking the wolves on patrols of a set perimeter. In the final week, the patrols extended further to include outside travel, aimed at acclimatising Fen and Arty to travel by car and refreshing their memory of the cottage and surrounding fields. They patrolled the perimeter of the land daily, re-establishing their territory. Then it was back to the barracks for more training and socialising exercises. Finally, they established that Marie, Rose, and Aston were higher up in the pack than Fen and Arty, although Daniel and his family had been unable to find the time to join them.

After all this hard work, it was no wonder Freya was delighted by the news that she had passed. She gave a loud whoop.

"What are you whooping about?' Marie asked, having just returned from signing the house contract. "You're not that pleased to be getting rid of me, are you?"

Freya gave her a hug.

"Of course not. I've just had the news that I've passed my training. Fen and Arty will be signed over to me after the passing-out ceremony. I'll have to take part in it. I hope you'll all be there to cheer me on."

Marie flung her arms round her mother.

"Oh, just try and stop us! That's wonderful news. You deserve recognition for all your dedication. Well done, Mum. I'll phone Daniel. Leave all the arrangements to me"

"Wonderful. But no noisy party. Keep it low key. Remember I'll be bringing Fen and Arty home at last, and they'll need peace and quiet to settle on their first night. A quiet dinner party, maybe?"

"Understood." Marie gave her mum a mock salute and received the flicked edge of a tea-towel from Freya for her cheek. Both women laughing delightedly.

Although she had completed her training successfully and was no longer required to live-in at the barracks or sleep in the kennel, Freya continued going into the army camp early every morning. The care and daily routine of Fen and Arty were still her responsibility, and it was more important than ever to maintain the bonds she had established with the wolves.

For the first time David would not be part of the process. He had done everything required of him to ensure the terms set by his client, the colonel, were met. Freya now understood how much she had come to rely on him. He had been by her side with gentle comfort in times of frustration and doubt and offered his blustering support in the face of the bullying scorn she had at times suffered. She had come to think of him, and value him, as a friend. Now she realised their paths had crossed for only a short time. The path ahead – the path she had chosen – was hers, not his.

She swallowed the lump in her throat, reining in the threatened tears, as she realised how much she would miss him. And to make matters worse, Marie had returned to Whitby to prepare for the move into her new home and the children had gone with her to help with the packing up of their old, rented house.

5

Wolf Woman

Freya was recognised at the sentry points now and was waved through, with a smile and, occasionally, a salute. How different from that first day when, overcome with trepidation, she had found David waiting for her and, unheeding of their brief acquaintance, had almost flung herself into his arms, so thankful was she at seeing his friendly face. Just as she had done so often over the years since her husband's death, she pushed aside the thoughts that threatened to weaken her resolve, burying them in the need to stay strong as she moved forward.

As the weeks sped past and the day of her passing out came closer, everything seemed to fall into place. Marie was settled in her new house, Aston was settling into his new school, while Rose was exercising her independence and preparing to head to university. It had been all go and Freya now relished the peace and tranquillity of being alone in the cottage, spending the summer evenings taking leisurely strolls around the garden or sitting with a glass of rosé beside the river, as the sun set.

On the day of the ceremony, Freya went to the kennels especially early. She wanted to give Fen and Arty an extra-long exercise session to keep them calm (really it was to allay her own nerves). Excitement buzzed among the cadets with whom she had trained and despite their age difference, she welcomed their banter and camaraderie. She was both surprised and amused to learn she been dubbed "The Wolf Woman".

"So, Wolf Woman!' one of them said. "While we'll be going on to suffer more of the verbal abuse from the sarge, what are your plans?"

Laughing, Freya replied, "Well, my plans were to take Fen and Arty and retire to a quiet life. But with a tag like Wolf Woman, maybe we should be taking to the air to fight crime, like a super-hero." With an extended arm reaching skywards, she imitated Superman.

Among the general laughter, several voices responded.

"Now that's something I'd like to see!"

"You'll need Kryptonite. I'll see if I can get you some."

Soon they had all dispersed to their various tasks. Freya was extra thorough as she groomed Fen and Arty, wanting them to look their best on their last day as members of the armed forces. After giving them their breakfast, she returned home to prepare herself for the coming event.

As the ceremony began, Freya, the last in the line as the only civilian, entered the parade ground with Fen and Arty either side of her. There was total silence as each recruit put their charge through their routine before being presented with their new insignia, promoting them from cadet to private. Freya was the only one handling two 'dogs' simultaneously and she silently prayed she wouldn't mess up and let everyone down. She needn't have worried. Major Winguard had socialised them to perfection and they had worked with him many times in the parade ring, so it should have been no surprise that they followed the routine flawlessly. Freya was moved to tears when they presented themselves to the major. Fen and Arty received, not only their discharge papers, but also medals of honour in recognition of their loyal and courageous service alongside Major Winguard in Afghanistan. Freya was also awarded a special commendation by Major Hodson.

"Ms Fraser, I will confess, I had my doubts as to your ability to complete the task you had set yourself. However, I am delighted to see you have proved me wrong. It was no easy task to take on the care of two animals who had lived and worked beside their former handler twenty-four hours a day in peace and war. They formed the closest bond I have ever seen between man and beast. You have earned their trust and if their loyalty is ever put to the test, I doubt you will find it lacking. I salute you, Ms Fraser, for your courage in taking on the care, not of two dogs, but of two full-blooded wolves."

The rest of the ceremony passed in an excited blur, as all the recruits posed for official passing-out photographs and Freya was encouraged to pose with them. Individual photographs followed for the official yearbook. Once more Freya was not allowed to escape from the ordeal. She posed for her photograph, standing proudly between Fen and Arty, as she idly fondled their ears. Dressed as she was in a grey trouser suit chosen specially, the three looked like a true pack.

Freya did not at that point join her family, who had watched the ceremony from the civilian gallery above the parade ground. She had explained in advance that she would take Fen and Arty home to make sure they were settled before the evening celebrations began. She arranged for her guests to follow and meet up at the cottage. As Freya loaded Fen and Arty into the car, she thought she couldn't have been happier. Nothing could top this day, she was certain. That is, she was certain – until she felt a hand placed lightly on her shoulder and, turning, she found David holding out a huge bouquet of the most beautiful flowers. They both spoke at the same time.

"I'm sorry," David said. "I didn't want to intrude, but I had to come."

"I thought you had washed your hands of me, having completed your duty," Freya blurted.

Their words jumbled together, and they laughed, not without some embarrassment.

"I have to dash to get my boys settled. Marie is hosting a dinner party later in my honour. You will come, won't you?" Freya tried to keep a pleading note from her tone.

David nodded. "She was kind enough to invite me, but I didn't want to impose further into your life. You've put up with me pushing myself forward long enough. But if you are certain, I would love to come."

"Why would you think it an imposition? I thought we had become friends. I've missed you."

"Then I'll look forward to seeing you this evening, Freya. Wild horses wouldn't keep me away."

He bent to plant a kiss on her cheek before she climbed into the car. As she drove off, she beeped the horn and called out of the window, "Thank you for the flowers. They're beautiful."

Freya's evening of celebration was one to remember, as her achievement was celebrated among her family and the new friends she had made over the past few months. The only blot was the absence of Daniel and his family. Marie passed on his apologies as she arrived.

"Daniel was feeling a bit green about the gills by the end of the ceremony. We all felt it was better for him not to come and risk spoiling your night. I'm sure he'll be feeling brighter tomorrow and will drop in to see you then."

Freya's maternal instincts kicked in immediately.

"Oh, what a shame! I'll just give him a call to see how he is and thank him for coming to the ceremony."

As Freya searched for her phone, she missed the frantic gestures and whispering that passed between Marie, David and Peter. Marre quickly grasped her mother's arm,

"He's fine mum, I spoke to Lisa a few minutes ago, he's all tucked up in bed, sleeping soundly. This is your night so let's celebrate."

6

Home Truths

Freya woke up the following morning happy and light-hearted. As she stretched beneath the duvet in preparation to starting her day, she realised she was content. For the first time in decades the struggles were behind her. She lived in a beautiful home in a beautiful setting. Her children were settled, her grandchildren strong, healthy and happy. There were no financial worries. She had Fen and Arty. She also had a man in her life whom she knew she could rely on as a good friend. She had a lot to be thankful for, and every reason to feel content.

But such bubbles of perfect happiness rarely last long. Freya's bubble burst barely minutes after she sat sipping her morning coffee, when Daniel arrived. He had no intention of beating about the bush with polite social niceties. Ignoring Freya's greeting and welcoming smile, he launched his attack.

"There is no easy or polite way to say this, Mother. I doubted the wisdom of you adopting two large dogs, but then I find the large dogs are, in fact, wolves. It's madness! I won't stand by and watch you put yourself in danger. You're alone here. You wouldn't stand a chance if they turned on you. The children wouldn't stand a chance if the wolves turned on them. Have you considered that?"

Freya was shocked but his reaction was what she had expected the minute he discovered Fen and Arty were wolves. She also knew that in his present mood, reasoning with him would only end in a shouting match which would achieve nothing. Instead, she remained calm and in control.

"Sit down, Daniel. Your concerns are valid and deserve to be answered. But Marie also deserves to hear the same explanation and I don't intend to repeat myself."

She reached for her phone. Marie answered almost immediately. Freya explained the situation and asked her to come over.

"Don't break any speeding records or cancel what you had planned, love, but as soon as you can get here would be appreciated."

"I'll be right there. Though Daniel will certainly not appreciate what I have to say. See you shortly, Mum."

Replacing the phone on the table, Freya stood up.

"Marie is on the way. Make yourself some breakfast if you want. I have to go to see to the boys. You can watch from the patio doors should you be interested, but don't come out. In your present mood you'll only unsettle them. They'll pick up on your mood and they need calm."

She didn't wait to hear his response. He would be better left alone to calm down, she thought, and she really did need to give her attention to Fen and Arty. It would not do to break their routine on their first day home.

The July sun was already warm, promising a hot day to come. Freya emptied her mind and let the beauty of her surroundings and the calm companionship of Fen and Arty soothe her spirit. She walked slowly, letting the wolves relish the smells of their territory, assuring themselves all was well. It was a meandering walk, along the riverbank, across the pastures and around the edge of the wood, before returning through the pastures to home.

Nearing the cottage, she saw Daniel watching from behind the patio doors, with Marie beside him. He did not look mollified, but Marie gave a wave. Freya waved back, before taking Fen and Arty through the service door into the garage. She gave them each their breakfast and a bowl of water before heading into the house. Poking her head into the dining room, she found Marie and Daniel sitting across from each other at the table. She gave Marie a quick hug.

"Thanks for coming. I'll be about half an hour. I need to brush the leaves and twigs from their coats. If either of you would like to make me a cup of tea and a light breakfast, it would be greatly appreciated."

Marie stood up, saying, "Daniel can make us all breakfast and I'll help you groom Fen and Arty. If you'd like some help with that?"

Freya hesitated, quickly weighing up whether Marie's offer of help would be a risk. It was only Fen and Arty's first full day at

38

home, but Marie knew how to behave around them. After all, all the socialisation exercises had been aimed at integrating her family into the pack order. She was confident it would be fine, but she needed to make sure that Marie was clear about what she was offering.

"That would be wonderful. But I need to be clear that you know the boys are wolves. I know I should have said something before now."

Marie grinned. "I've known for a while, Mum. Aston was convinced from the start that they were wolves, though I put it down to his imagination at first. Then there were the socialisation skills we had to learn. A bit excessive for dogs, I thought. In the end I asked Peter about it and reluctantly he told me."

Marie noticed her mother's raised eyebrow and gave her a playful nudge.

"Aw, don't blame him for giving up your secret. He'd have been very foolish to keep it from me. Come on. Let's get the boys cleaned up, so we can eat. Full Yorkshire for me, Danny, and don't burn the toast."

Silently, Daniel watched as his mother and sister headed to the garage, then, after only a brief hesitation, he headed to the kitchen to cook breakfast.

With Marie's help it didn't take long to groom the boys. The dry weather meant the leaves and twigs brushed out of their coats easily and they were not muddy. Freya was pleased that they had accepted Marie as easily as Marie had accepted them. In no time their task was done. Fen and Arty were returned to their kennel and settled down to sleep. Freya and Marie returned to the house where the smell of a cooked breakfast was more than a reward for their dutiful attention to the wolves.

Breakfast passed pleasantly enough, and Daniel listened to Freya's explanation quietly. But it was all downhill from there. His concerns were not so easily dealt with as Marie's. He had always been stubborn and reluctant to accept his opinion could be flawed in any way. As Freya finished speaking, he turned to Marie.

"There, you heard her. She's obsessed with a tree, to the point that she sells the house Dad worked so hard for and moves here to the middle of nowhere. And furthermore, she's prepared to put us and the children in danger from a pack of adopted wolves in order to do so. We must put a stop to this for her own safety. You must see that, Marie. She's not thinking rationally."

Both Freya and Marie were astounded by the speed at which the affable son and brother had turned assassin, if only to Freya's reputation. Marie replied instantly,

"Shut up, Danny, and don't speak again until you've taken a dose of loperamide hydrochloride. It will put a stop to the diarrhoea you're spouting!"

She would have said more, but Freya, putting a hand on her arm, spoke up for herself.

"It may suit you to speak about me rather than to me, Daniel, but I will remind you that whatever you think, I am fully compos mentis. I know you loved your father and rightly so. I loved him too. You were a child when he died, and I protected you as much as I could from the chaos he left behind."

Daniel, furious now, interrupted her.

"You protected us? Dad protected us and gave us everything. You plunged us into poverty and raised us as paupers practically."

Freya was deeply shocked and hurt by Daniel's words. But she kept her poise and resumed what she intended to say.

"As I was saying, you were a child when he died. But you're not a child now, Daniel, and the harsh reality is this. Your father was a good man, but, as I discovered after he died, he was far from a saint. He was a gambler. He had mortgaged the house to the hilt, and he had reneged on the debts he owed. That's why we were plunged into poverty after he died. To prevent the house being repossessed, I had to take on his debts and work my fingers to the bone to keep the roof over our heads. No, we did not have the same lifestyle we had enjoyed, but that lifestyle had been funded by gambling and debt. I made sure you lacked for none of the essentials, but I couldn't pay the bills if I bought luxuries. This is not about scoring points over your father. It's about the brutal truth I did my best to shield you from."

Daniel's unexpected animosity and the need to rake up the struggles of the past proved too much for Freya. Pushing back her chair, she left the room quickly before the tears started, muttering, "Give me a minute" as she excused herself.

Daniel remained silent, but Marie hurried after her mother, saying over her shoulder, "I always knew you could be an idiot, Daniel, but I never knew you could be such a bully. You make me sick."

By the time Freya and Marie returned to the cottage, Daniel had left.

"He's scuttled off with his tail between his legs," Marie commented, after looking out of the window to see his car had gone.

Freya wasn't so sure. She knew Daniel too well. He was like a terrier at a rat's nest he just wouldn't let it go. However, she hid her concern from Marie.

"You get off too, love. Unless you need to ask me anything?"

"No questions from me. We're your children, not your keepers, and you don't need to answer to us. I'll just have a cup of tea before I go."

Freya knew Marie's desperate need for a cup of tea was merely a ruse to enable her to ensure Freya was recovered from Daniel's visit. Marie had always been a blessing. Daniel, on the other hand, had always been a trial. Maybe the awful revelations of the morning explained why, she thought.

7

Pebbles Thrown in a Pool

Two days later a local newspaper ran a story on Freya's purchase of Sentinel Cottage, with a brief history of the Sentinel and general area. It was headed by an old picture of the Sentinel, obviously sourced from the archives somewhere. An old man stood beside the great tree with two dogs beside him. Sheep dogs probably, but it was hard to tell. The photograph was old and faded. There was no caption to say who the man was, but Freya guessed it must be a member of Major Winguard's family. Perhaps it was the colonel? The article was unremarkable, but it sparked a chain of events that caused ripples like a pebble dropped into a pool.

Firstly, Aston's teacher, Miss Carey, picked up on it, as Aston had been full of pride in his grandmother's "celebrity" status, as he saw it. She telephoned Marie to run her idea past her.

"I do hope there will be no objections, but I'm thinking a class project on the history of the Sentinel during the school holidays would be a wonderful way to integrate Aston more fully in his new school and help him maintain friendships out of school. Do you think your mother would mind?"

"I shouldn't think so," Marie replied. "But it depends on how intrusive you think it may be. Thirty-six kids with packed lunches and cameras descending on her property may not be a good plan. It may be best if you speak to her directly."

"Thanks, I'll do that, and don't worry about the number of children involved. Even in the large city schools, numbers are capped below that. We are talking much smaller numbers." Miss Carey had promised before hanging up the phone.

Following Miss Carey's call, Freya found herself entangled on all sides. She was adamant that the children could not, under any circumstances, invade the Sentinel's field, but agreed they could take photographs of the great oak from her front lawn. She also consented to the class (in fact there were only eleven children to accommodate) having their lunch there. It had to be by appointment, however, and be carefully managed.

"That's ever so kind of you, Ms Fraser. Dare I push you a little further? Would you consider giving a talk to the class on the history of the Sentinel and the land your cottage is sited upon? I believe it's the remnant of a Viking settlement. The children would be fascinated." Miss Carey hoped her own enthusiasm would communicate to Freya, but she was to be disappointed.

"I would be fascinated myself, Miss Carey, as I know nothing about the history of the Sentinel or the land. I am the least suited of anyone to give a talk on the subject. So, I have to decline, I'm afraid."

But Miss Carey didn't give up easily.

"Oh! What a wonderful opportunity then for you to do some research in preparation for your talk. Just think what you could discover, and you could support Aston with his project. Would that not be too good an opportunity to miss?"

Freya felt she was being coerced and she didn't like it.

"Miss Carey, you have my permission to arrange a visit here for the children, and that is as far as I am prepared to go. Naturally I will support my grandson in whatever way I can, but that will be between Aston and myself. I will not be preparing to give a talk, so … if that is all?"

"I understand, Ms Fraser. Perhaps we can take a rain check on the talk. Can I pencil you in for two weeks' time? You may feel better prepared then."

"We can certainly agree your class visit for that time frame, but it will take us through to the start of the summer holidays as I'm sure you are aware," said Freya. "But I will not be giving a talk to your class or anyone else. Thank you for calling, Miss Carey. Goodbye."

Freya didn't know if she was annoyed or amused. She opted for amused and gave a laugh, thinking, "You may be pushy, Miss Carey, but you're no match for my stubbornness."

However, Miss Carey's suggestion of researching the topic had merit, Freya concluded. She and Aston could work together. Marie had invited her for tea that evening. She would discuss it with them then.

Freya hated it when her family treated her as either a source of amusement or a poor old soul who was on the verge of mental incompetence. Following Daniel's accusations, she was particularly sensitive now. The latest incident was sparked later that evening when she suggested to Aston a trip to the library to kick-start their project.

"I've got loads of stuff off Google, Nan," said Aston. "I don't need books."

"Of course, you'll need books," Freya retorted. "And I'll certainly need them since I don't have access to a computer."

"Just buy a computer, Nan," Rose suggested, with over-emphasised patience. "Nobody uses libraries anymore. Everything's online."

"I could do that easily enough, but it won't do me any good. Cable doesn't stretch to Sentinel Cottage. There is no satellite, not even an aerial, so I can't even use the T.V. let alone install the internet on a computer." Freya's response was delivered with equal patience.

That stunned them to silence for a few moments. Then Marie, business-like, said, "That can't be right, Mum. I'll investigate it tomorrow, and get it sorted. You need your TV and a computer. In the meantime, you and Aston can work from here and you're always welcome to come to watch our telly. You know that."

Freya knew Marie meant what she said. She reached across the table to touch her daughter's cheek.

"Thanks, love"

Later, as she was saying her goodbyes, Aston handed her a pile of papers.

"I've printed everything off for you, Nan. To give you time to read through it. And maybe you can come next Friday, and we can go through it then, if that's OK?"

She gave him a hug. "That's brilliant. Thank you. I'll see you Friday."

Climbing into the car, she chuckled to herself. Her grandson had just set her homework!

Once home, she tended to Fen and Arty, enjoying their walk around what she laughingly called "The Homestead". It was full summer, but in the evening drizzle there was a chill in the air, though it certainly didn't bother the wolves. Fen walked close to Freya's side, while Arty brought up the rear. They followed the boundary of the river before heading around the perimeter of Lucky's Grove, then across the pasture back to the house. The small woodland should have offered a natural habitat for the wolves, but Freya found it curious that they never entered it but always stuck to the perimeter. In the growing darkness, however, she was happy to avoid the interior with its tangled roots and its damp, mulchy floor.

With her animal care duty done, Freya settled the wolves for the night and locked up the cottage. She set the log burning fire and ran herself a bath, phoning David while it filled. He answered on the third ring.

"Freya! To what do I owe the pleasure? Is everything OK?"

"Everything's fine, David. I'm sorry to call so late. I just need pointing in the right direction for the library. I'm helping Aston with some research on the history of the Sentinel and thought the local history of the area would be a good place to start."

"Sorry to be the bearer of bad news, Freya, but we don't have a local library anymore. Not as a building anyway. There is a library bus. It comes once a month and will call by arrangement to the outlying area. Hang on. I'll just find the number."

Muffled sounds came down the line as David presumably headed off, but he returned quickly, reeling off the number to Freya. She thanked him, apologising again for disturbing him, and was about to hang up when he added, "You may do better to try the library and record office in Northallerton. A lot of their database is online. York Record Office also has a lot of information online. Trawling the Net will save you the hassle of trawling the shelves and save travel time."

Freya sighed inwardly. Everyone was obsessed with the internet and assumed it was as much an essential of life as breathing oxygen. It would be ungracious to be quarrelsome, however, so she refrained from mentioning her lack, simply determining to visit Northallerton the next day. Hoping the record office would be open on a Saturday, she said her goodbyes.

"Thanks, David. I knew I could tap into your local knowledge. You've been a great help."

By the time next Friday came around Freya had absorbed information from all the print-outs Aston had given her as well as adding a whole plethora gained from the record office. She could barely contain her excitement in sharing it with him and the rest of her family.

"You'd never guess, but the Sentinel goes back further than Domesday Book! I have a Saxon land holding record showing it as standing on what is named as the land of Heimdall in 946. Of course, Sentinel cottage did not exist then but what is now the boundaries of Sentinel Cottage are clearly traceable, but it looks like the original boundary of Heimdall's land extended further to the north and east. It mentions a cluster of dwellings which I think may be the settlement, but it's a bit vague, so we'll have to find out more." In her excitement, Freya had gushed out her information in a muddle of fact and her own speculation, hardly pausing to allow Aston to assimilate what she was saying until she paused to take a breath.

"Who was Heimdall?" Aston asked

Before Freya could reply, Marie interrupted. "It's generally considered polite to say hello when you come in, Mother, before you go into full flow of hogging the conversation." She was smiling and reaching to hug her mother as she spoke, but it was a rebuke, nevertheless.

"You're absolutely right, my love. Forgive me. I'm just so excited! How are things with you?"

"I've been busy too, on your behalf. Help me set the table and I'll tell you what you need to do to get the internet installed."

Before following Marie, Freya handed her collection of papers to Aston.

"I'm not sure exactly who Heimdall was, but we'll find out. The lady at the record office suggested he was probably a former owner of the land, most likely a Viking, though by 946, most Viking lands had fallen under the control of the Saxon control again. She is going to look out more records and send me transcriptions of what she finds. I'm not sure if they'll be here before your assignment is due though. I'd better go and help your mum. We'll go over them later." She kissed her grandson on the top of his head to seal her promise.

As usual Marie had cooked a fine meal, over which she told Freya all about what might be needed to get the internet installed at Sentinel Cottage.

"It would be possible to get the cable company to lay a cable out to the cottage. But it would take time for them to get the necessary permissions from the council and possibly other land holders, and the cost is nigh on astronomical."

46

"How much is astronomical?" asked Freya.

"They were talking tens of thousands. But our phones work at the cottage, so it must be able to receive a wi-fi signal. If you buy a good PC and mobile internet, that may work straight away. It's worth a try, considering the saving you'd make."

"Well, that sounds like a plan. Are you free to come with me tomorrow and see what's available?"

"Yes, no problem. if we can go early. I'm seeing Peter in the afternoon. I wanted to ask if you would have Aston overnight. Rose is staying with friends."

"I'll have my buddy any time you want. Now, I'll help Aston clear away the supper dishes, then we can check out the land boundary document and the possible settlement. What do you think, Aston?"

"That will be cool."

With their chore completed, Freya and Aston sat at the table as they pored over the boundary map. While it had been nowhere near the acreage associated with the present-day landed gentry, Heimdall's land had been substantially larger than the remnants now owned by Freya, with the Sentinel clearly marked as standing in the centre. Several small dwellings were shown scattered about the opposite bank of the river, which curiously appeared to run where the road was today. The Sentinel was shown standing alone, north of the river with the dwellings, and the grove on the south bank.

" Nan, while I'm staying with you over the weekend, can we use this document to try and trace the original boundary? We can take Fen and Arty with us."

"Absolutely. We can do it tomorrow afternoon then we can go into York on Sunday, to the Jorvik Centre, soak up the Viking atmosphere and get some lunch. What do you say?"

"I say YAY!" Aston flung himself at Freya, winding his arms around her neck to give her a hug.

They achieved so much over the weekend. The PC and mobile internet were installed and although Aston complained it was too slow, it worked well enough to please Freya. David joined them for the exploration of the boundaries. He and Aston took the land record and ventured further afield, beyond Freya's land, where Fen and Arty were not permitted to go.

A bright but weak sun made golden ripples on the river, and Freya sat at the water's edge with the wolves, excited and anxious to hear whether they would discover anything. It seemed an age before they returned, but at last she saw Aston waving and smiling as he ran towards her. David, also smiling, followed at more of an amble. Fen and Arty stood, alert, as Aston yelled, "We found it, Nan, we found it." He flung himself down beside Freya, while Fen and Arty joyously welcomed him back to the pack.

"Stand down, Private Fen. At rest!" Freya repeated the command for Arty.

Although she was confident now that the wolves recognised Aston as part of their pack, and knew Aston was well schooled in how to behave around them, she was ever vigilant, not wanting excessive excitement to spill over into rough play or over-confidence.

She took her three charges to meet David, as he breathlessly made his way across the field towards them.

"Good work, my intrepid explorer," she laughed as she linked his arm. "I think you've earned yourself a drink before supper."

Supper was a quick one-pot chasseur, which, having been prepared earlier, cooked away on its own, while Freya and Aston fed, groomed and bedded Fen and Arty down. David, a well-watered scotch in hand, played around on the new computer, uploading the photographs taken of the boundary marks and linking them with the boundary record before sketching a very rough map

The land was unenclosed (the characteristic dry-stone walls would not appear on the landscape for many centuries past the Norse age).

"The scale seems way off unless the river was diverted at some point Still, it clearly shows the lie of the land. The hills on the horizon line can easily be traced. Check out the photos we took today. It's also clear the settlement itself would have been across the river. So, the land extended further south as well as to the west and east." David was confident in his assessment. He was after all an estate agent and use to dealing with land boundaries.

Aston's excitement bubbled up. "If you had enough money, Nan, you could buy the land back. Heimdall would be happy if you did that."

Freya hid a smile as she replied, "I'm sure Heimdall would be over the moon, but he's not here to help care for it, sadly. I have enough land for my needs."

"It's not such a bad idea, you know, Freya," said David, thoughtfully. "Your original fears over the expansion of the new town are proving right. If you could buy the land, it would protect you from any encroachment that would detract from your tranquillity here. And ensure the safety of the Sentinel. Who knows what damage heavy diggers could cause to its root system?"

"Do you think that's going to happen or is it just rumours?" Freya asked, nervously.

"I'm not trying to frighten you, Freya. There are certainly more rumours flying about, but with some truth. Expansion plans are underway."

"Then let's not hang about," she said, surprising herself by making an instant decision. "Better safe than sorry. Though what I'm going to do with more land, I don't know! Can you handle things, David? Make enquiries and negotiate terms, and we'll take it from there." She paused for a moment. "You know, this takes panic buying to a whole new level! Aston, keep this to yourself for now, OK?"

"Well, I wasn't expecting to be taking part in a council of war," said David. "But our lips are sealed, aren't they, lad?" He nudged Aston, who nodded enthusiastically.

Freya poured them each a drink – lemonade for Aston, watered scotch for David and a white wine for herself – and they drank a toast to the protection of Heimdall's land and to the Sentinel (proposed by Aston), before David took his leave.

"We need an early night too, Aston," said Freye. "We've an early start tomorrow. Do you want some supper first?"

"Just a bowl of cornflakes with hot milk, please, Nan."

In less than half an hour Aston was settled in bed. and on the verge of sleep, Freya wasn't long behind.

She dreamed.

8

Freya's First Dream

In the smoke-filled room a woman, perhaps in her late thirties, spooned broth into two bowls, speaking as she did so.

"Erik, you and Bjorn must eat before going to the meeting. It is not much but at least it will warm and line your belly before you go into the cold."

Erik, her husband, sat on a long bench built into the fabric of the longhouse, running along each of the four walls. He was pulling on his trousers. Considering the weather, he was glad that despite the new fashion of separate hosen, he had seen elsewhere, here they retained the traditional full trouser with gussets to the back and front for the freer movement needed to man the farm or the ships. He stood to fasten the leather thongs that held them up.

"The boy will eat. I am not hungry, Astrid, you have mine. Save the rest for the younger children."

Astrid poured the uneaten broth back into the pot that hung over the open fire on a tripod. Then she went to her husband as he was pulling his tunic over his head. Its tailored cut showed off his muscular body. She smiled into his deep blue eyes.

"If you won't eat, at least let me braid your hair. You look like a Wildman."

Erik laughed, pulling her into his embrace.

"Then I am a fitting match for my wild woman," he retorted, giving her a quick kiss.

She pushed him on to the bench, laughing. "Sit!"

Drawing a comb from her pocket, she pulled back his copper-coloured hair and, ignoring his pained cries, combed until it was tangle free. Then she deftly braided it into a long plait running from the top of his head, revealing the short, shaved sides and back. Satisfied, she turned her attention, and her comb, to her eldest son, leaving Erik to finish dressing.

At sixteen Bjorn was a younger version of Erik: the same copper glint in his hair, the same intense look in his eyes and the same stubborn set to his square jawline. Like all youths approaching manhood, he was resentful of his mother's ministrations. Nevertheless, he sat while she completed her task, combing and braiding his hair into the same style as his father.

"I don't need fussing like a baby, Mother," he said. He stood to pull on his cloak over his woollen jerkin, adding his belt which held the tools of his trade. Astrid ignored his protests.

"Put your hood on too. I don't want you catching a chill and infecting the little ones."

As father and son stood side by side, each a version of the other, dressed identically, she cupped the face of her son in her hands.

"You are growing fast into manhood and are more your father's son now. Pay heed to his teaching and honour him, but never forget, I will always be your mother. Now go, both of you, and may Odin give you wisdom this day."

Bjorn headed towards the door, but Erik delayed. He filled a bowl with the broth, handing it to Astrid.

"Did you think I wouldn't notice that you did not eat? We need you to stay strong instead of sickening for lack of food. I will not leave until I know that bowl is empty, and the contents lie in your belly."

Astrid complied, knowing it would do no good to refuse. Then she watched from the door as her husband led their son towards the Thingstead, the meeting house. They were joined by other men as they walked, among them Roar and Knud, Erik's younger brothers. She looked around at the group of houses, smoke pouring from the smoke holes in their wet, dripping roofs, each one offering protection and warmth to her friends, neighbours and family. From their doorways, other women were doing the same as Astrid, watching as their menfolk trudged through the muddy street, over wattle hurdles laid flat to form a footpath to the large building at the centre of the village. Critical decisions were to be made in the Thingstead that would determine the survival of this village which had been the home of Astrid's growing family since she had married Erik, almost eighteen years ago

Inside the Thingstead, it was smoky and dimly lit. A few fire brands had been strategically placed, but the wood on the fire was damp, providing neither light nor warmth. The men gathered on the benches around the walls, while the three elders, Gothi Njal, Gothi

51

Birger and Gothi Skarde the Black (so named for his once black hair, now more grey than black) took their places, standing in the centre of the large room. They each wore a long cloak of tanned hide and carried a staff carved with runes, to mark their rank. Erik and Bjorn sat flanked by Roar and Knud. Skarde opened the meeting.

"My brothers, friends and neighbours, let us begin by asking the Allfather to guide us with his wisdom. We have passed through unprecedented times. The harshness of the winter and spring did not allow us to plant our crops. What little we could get into the ground has been washed away by the summer of rain. You do not need me to tell you this."

Njal stepped froward to take up were Skarde had broken off.

"We stand on a precipice. Starvation awaits us and our families unless we can find a way to ward it off. We are open to your suggestions."

Troels Thoreson, one of the younger men, stood to say his piece.

"I think we should go raiding. We won't starve. We can take what food we need and maybe get riches too. It has to be better than facing another winter like the last. What do you say?"

"That may be the choice that suits you," Birger responded. "You may well get rich. Or you may get yourself killed and have a death more merciful than starvation. But it will not help your younger brothers and sisters, your mother, or the rest of this village. Remember, we are not here to serve ourselves, but our community."

Another man stood.

"Perhaps it would be better if each family struck out on their own. With fewer people it may be easier to find enough food to get through the winter."

"Perhaps, but where would they go?' Birger spoke once again. "Where would they find food and shelter in the coming winter? The threat of starvation is not one faced by us alone. The winter without end struck most of the Northlands and all are facing the same problem."

Erik stood.

"It is well known that I have three trading ships. If families wish to leave the village to find a better life, they will need to travel further afield. Angleland perhaps, or Irland. I will put my ships at their disposal, captained by myself and my son Bjorn, and if they agree, my brothers, Roar and Knud. But first I would be prepared for my ships to go out and see what supplies we can find at the trading centres between here and Jutland. I will need every able-bodied man to crew them, as well as each family to contribute what they can to the trading fund. What say you all?"

If there were any dissenting voices, they were lost in the roar of approval.

As the scene changed, time must have passed. It could have been hours or days, but Astrid, along with most of the village, stood by the water's edge, five-year-old Freyja clinging to her skirts, while Thurid, her eldest daughter, stood between her younger brothers, Ulf and Gorm. Despite the mud, and the threat of even more rain, there was a carnival atmosphere among the gathered throng who waited to see Erik's ships leave. The trading party gave them hope, and with hope came joy. In other times there would have been a feast and the mead would have flowed, but in this time of threatened famine, nothing could be spared, save a cup for each of the captains and a single jug to be passed around each of the ship's crews.

"They're coming."

Thurid, her arms around her brothers, hugged the boys to her as they watched Erik and Bjorn swing from the ship and head towards them. From all three ships other men were doing the same, to say farewell to their families.

As Erik drew nearer, Ulf broke free from Thurid's grasp and ran to meet his father.

"Take me with you. If Bjorn can go, so can I. I am old enough."

Erik gripped his son by his shoulders.

"Bjorn is coming because as the eldest he must learn his trade. You will be my arm and my eyes to protect your mother, sisters, and younger brother in my absence. You will stand in for me as protector and shield of the family. I would put my trust in no other/ You are the Wolf, are you not?"

Reluctantly Ulf nodded his acceptance. Erik went to each of his children, imparting his wisdom and his love to each before he came to Astrid. She held him close, putting both her arms about his neck.

53

"I will miss you every minute of every day," she whispered.

"And I you. But I will be back in two weeks, three at most. Then I will be handing over the ships to Bjorn and will stay by your side. It will not be long."

He stood back, about to take his leave, but she pulled on his sleeve.

"I have made you something to carry with you." She rummaged in her pocket, pulling out a small square of material, stitched with an image of the God Njord, ruler of the sea and the protector of ships and seafarers. She handed it to her husband.

He looked at it lovingly, before carefully folding it and pushing it inside his jerkin, where it lay next to his heart. There was no time to say more. A beating drum signalled the approach of the Gothi, coming to give a blessing to the ships and crews for a successful endeavour. All along the line, men made their final farewells and took their places on the ships. Erik and Bjorn were no exception.

Silence fell on the villagers as the drumbeat grew louder. The Gothi, their faces painted for the ritual, walked solemnly behind the drummer. Astrid and her children watched with fascination as they passed. With their faces stark white, lips bright red and eyes of black, they looked fierce, magical, powerful creatures of the world beyond. Behind them, three small goats, skinny and half starved, were tethered to one long pole. Guided on each side by two cloaked figures, they were being led to sacrifice. A horn blew, summoning the three captains, Erik, Roar and Knud, from their ships to stand before the Gothi. The drumbeat continued but quieter now. As one, the three Gothi raised their arms to invoke the aid of the gods.

"Mighty Thor, ruler of the skies and all things therein, hold back the tempests to protect these ships and men from harm. Grant a fresh wind to fill the sails and ease their journey. May storms do them no harm. We implore you to aid their journey with all that is good and valuable to their mission.

"Njord, ruler of the oceans and seas. Grant your protection from the monsters of the deep who would seek to lure them to their destruction. Send the waves that will carry them boldly onwards and return them safely to us.

"Mighty Thor, Njord, Lord of the Seas, accept this sacrifice. These goats may not be the best you could expect, but they are the best we have to offer."

The pole to which the goats were tethered was raised, suspending the goats in mid-air. The ties around their scrawny necks tightened as they wriggled and kicked, fighting to break free. The Gothi were merciful, slitting the throats of the captives quickly. There was a collective gasp as blood spurted. The captains knelt, their faces upturned to allow the goats' lifeblood to spill on to them. Now the drum was beating loudly once more. The captains stood, each taking the still-warm body of a goat to be strung from the prow of their ship for the blessings to be carried with them.

Astrid, along with everybody else, began to sing. They kept singing, on the muddy bankside, until the ships had set sail up the Joterlandshaff and were lost from view.

9

Family Secrets

"Wake up, Nan! We'll be late for Jorvik, and Fen and Arty have been howling for ages."

Aston was shaking Freya awake, jumping on the bed all the while.

Sleep-befuddled and still partially in the clutches of her dream, Freya reluctantly pushed the covers off, as the wolves howled once more.

"Good God! Something must be disturbing them. Stay here, Aston, while I check what it is."

As she pushed her feet into her slippers and pulled on her dressing gown, all vestiges of sleep and the dream vanished. She was far too concerned for Fen and Arty. Speeding down the stairs and through the house, she opened the door into the garage, flicking on the light. All was quiet. The wolves were sleeping. Fen opened an eye, gave a lazy yawn, then stood to greet her.

Cautiously, Freya looked around the room. Nothing seemed to have been disturbed. She checked the garage door. It was still locked from the inside. She found it to be the same at the garden door.

"So, which of you has been howling at the moon in your dreams?" she asked as she approached the two wolves. Arty, now having woken, was standing beside his brother. She smiled at them.

"My apologies for disturbing your rest, but it wouldn't have happened if you had not disturbed mine. At ease, Privates Fen and Arty. I'll be back soon."

As the wolves settled once more, Freya returned to the house, shouting up the stairs to Aston.

"Everything's OK. You can come down now. I'll make some tea and toast."

Aston leapt down the stairs.

"Why were they howling? Are they hurt?"

"They're both fine. Nothing more dramatic than a dreaming wolf," Freya laughed, and Aston joined in.

56

They planned their day sitting around the table in their PJs, enjoying the warm toast with honey.

"We can exercise Fen and Arty and sort them out first, then get ourselves ready. Do you want a proper breakfast before we leave," Freya asked, "or shall we stop off in Ripon and grab something there?"

"This will do me, I'm stuffed," Aston replied, patting his belly to prove his point, "We can take some snacks with us though."

Two hours later they were on their way, with half the contents of Freya's pantry to cover Aston's "snacks". He was tucking into them well before they passed through Masham to join the A6108. In between chewing, crunching, and slurping, Aston chatted away, excitedly.

"I'll have the best assignment, won't I, Nan? Have you been to Jorvik before? What will we see?"

Freya hid a smile.

"Whoa! One question at a time. I'm certain your assignment will be as brilliant as you are. But this will be my first visit to Jorvik too, so I've no idea what to expect. I'm sure it will be amazing, though."

Aston returned to his snacks, as Freya concentrated on navigating her way through the Leeming Lane roundabouts and on to the A1 south towards York. Once on the motorway, she returned to her conversation with Aston.

"When your mum and Uncle Daniel were younger, their school had a daytrip to Jorvik, but I couldn't afford to pay for them to go. I always meant to take them another time, but I never had two pennies spare, so they missed out, regrettably."

"Is that why Uncle Daniel is angry with you?" asked Aston, his head tilted to the side.

Freya had not seen or spoken to Daniel since his outburst following the passing out ceremony, so she was surprised that Aston was aware of it. She wasn't going to dump her concerns on him, however, or let it ruin the day, so she responded lightly.

"I don't think Uncle Daniel is truly angry. I think he was just taken by surprise when he found out that Fen and Arty are wolves. He'll calm down and see sense."

"He won't. He's really, really angry, Nan. He asked Mum to help get you put away. He said that you are madder than a hatter and only an insane old woman would think it was OK to keep wolves as pets."

"What?" Freya was too shocked to say anything else.

"Mum had a big argument with him," Aston continued. "And Peter told him that whatever he was planning, he could forget it, because you are the most stable and courageous woman he has ever met."

"Good for Peter!" Freya muttered.

"Peter said that you had been given intensive training to handle the wolves and had undergone testing every step of the way. And he told Uncle Daniel that any move he made against you, he made against the British army, and he would lose."

Freya gripped the steering wheel so tight her knuckles were white. Her stomach churned. She had had no idea Daniel was continuing to pursue his threats, and it shocked her. By a stroke of luck, they entered Poppleton just then, and she made her way to the Park and Ride. She didn't trust herself to drive further. A coffee and a bus ride would give her time to collect her thoughts without upsetting Aston. She tried to keep her voice light.

"Come on. We'll get a quick drink, then take the bus the rest of the way. It's not far now."

She was deeply disturbed at the thought that her relationship with Daniel was in such dire straits, but she was an expert at pushing her worries to one side and hiding them from the world. By the time they alighted from the bus in York, she gave the appearance of being a light-hearted Nan enjoying a day out with her grandson, as she and Aston chatted excitedly about the day ahead.

10

Vikings

On Coppergate they almost walked past the entrance to the Jorvik Viking Centre, it was so unprepossessing. There was no indication they were about to enter a different world that ran beneath the modern shopping centre, the world of tenth-century Viking Jorvik.

Freya found the interactive display of the original dig, housed beneath a glass floor, fascinating, but, at first, didn't share her enthusiasm. There was only one place he wanted to be and that was on board the time-capsule, a ride that carried them "back in time" to explore the reconstructed city based on the archaeological finds of the Coppergate dig. But before they could reach it, a deep voice spoke up.

"You look like a young warrior who would be interested in the tools and weapons found at Jorvik. Come with me. My name is Rollo."

The speaker was a costumed member of the staff. He directed his words to Aston, but he winked and smiled at Freya. With his long reddish-blond hair, piercing blue eyes and beard decorated with rings, he looked every inch a Viking, especially with his axe tucked into his belt. Aston was enthralled. He followed Rollo without checking with Freya, who trailed behind, listening.

"My name's Aston. Did you know Erik? He's dead now, but he lives in a tree called the Sentinel by my Nan's cottage. My Nan has his wolves, Fen and Arty."

Rollo was skilled at handling the ramblings of children, though he glanced at Freya with a raised eyebrow and a questioning look as he replied.

"I have known two men called Erik. One was my friend, the other was my king, Erik Bloodaxe, King of Jorvik. I don't know any who live in a tree."

Freya said quickly, with an affectionate ruffle of Aston's hair, "He has lived and breathed Viking history ever since I moved into my cottage earlier this year. It's part of what was a Viking settlement. I do have an ancient tree that is called the Sentinel, which

59

dates to the time the settlement was occupied. I also have two wolves which formerly belonged to the previous owner of the cottage – a member of the British army, not a Viking." She paused, smiling at Rollo, before continuing, "Aston has an excellent imagination, which sometimes weaves the past and present together, not always accurately."

Rather than responding to Freya, Rollo turned back to Aston.

"Aston, you may be a bard or a seer rather than a warrior, or perhaps all three. These are the weapons."

He crouched down, quickly followed by Aston. Beneath the glass floor, replicas of the weapons that had been excavated were shown in situ. Rollo was clearly an expert in his field and an excellent educator. For the next twenty minutes he kept Aston and Freya enthralled.

When Rollo stood again, indicating their time with him was over, he reached down to help Freya up. Her knees had locked, and she had pins and needles. She gave him a rueful smile of thanks.

"It's been a pleasure meeting you both," Rollo said. Then he seemed to hesitate before adding, "There is a children's re-enactment camp in a few weeks. I think Aston would love it. There should be a leaflet tucked inside your guidebook with all the details."

"Will you be there, Rollo?" Aston asked, latching on to the idea enthusiastically.

"I will be there, along with many of the Great Army. We will teach you many of the skills a young warrior should master."

"Then I'll see you there. Nan will sort it all out."

Freya shook Rollo's hand, smiling. "Thank you so much for your time today. He's loved it. I'll be in touch about the camp."

She and Aston made their way back to the time-capsules.

"Wilkom in Jorvik."

A Viking animatronic greeted them in old Norse as they boarded the time-capsule, while his dog barked its own welcome. It was a nice touch, Freya thought, as she and Aston settled into the ride. Then the countdown in time began, taking them backwards through the historic timeline of UK history, stopping eventually in the tenth century.

The ride moved amidst dimly lit houses made of wattle, representing the types of domestic dwelling of the Viking era which would have given shelter to families, and where children would have played games while mothers did what all mothers have dome since time immemorial. Fathers sat outside the doors, passing on their skills to their sons. Dogs barked, cats loitered, chickens clucked, while pigs grunted and snuffled in the dirt of a wattle-walled pen. There was even the animated representation of a man using the toilet, which made Aston laugh and Freya almost heave with the authentic smells that accompanied it. Aston clicked away with his phone as they continued to pass through the workshops of artisans such as the shoemaker, the wood turner, the dyer and many more. Finally, they passed through the busy marketplace, where the leatherworker sold his wares and housewives renewed their pots and pans and stocked up their larders at the butchers. It was crowded, noisy and smelly, but totally fascinating.

Even so, Freya was glad to emerge from the ride into the clean lines and displays of the artefacts, although the lighting remained dim.

"Nan! Nan! Come and look! I've found the weapons Rollo showed us. They're all cleaned up."

Freya was pulled away from the beautiful pieces of amber jewellery she had been looking at, to follow Aston to a case displaying a range of knives and a sword.

"Wow! They're very impressive. I've never thought about so many different uses a knife could have." Freya peered into the display case which showed knives for eating, knives for craft work and other occupational uses as well as for weapons.

When she managed to usher Aston on and they were once more on modern Coppergate, they headed to the gift shop, which was separate to the main attraction. They emerged with gifts of amber and silver jewellery for Marie and Rose, a replica Viking boardgame for Aston, and a purchase Freya kept secret from Aston. She knew he would love it but wasn't sure he was old enough for it yet. It was a working replica of a small folding penknife. She would have to discuss it with Marie. It could always be put away for the future. She had no doubt it would remind Aston of the day he had met Rollo, no matter when he received it.

It seemed very strange to return to the Coppergate of the twenty-first century. They had lunch at a restaurant beside the river, followed by a trip on the boat. Aston pretended they were on a Viking trading ship, much to the amusement of the other passengers. The sun was shining high in the sky and the afternoon was hot as they disembarked. Freya bought them both an ice-cream which they ate as they made their way to catch the bus back to Poppleton. Soon they had collected the car and were on their way home.

By the time Marie arrived, with Peter, to collect Aston, Freya was preparing a light evening meal. While it cooked, she poured prosecco into three glasses and home-made lemonade into a fourth. She handed a tray with drinks to Marie, while Peter was entrusted with a dish of salad.

"Aston's outside with Fen and Arty. You know the drill. I'll be out in a minute."

Fen and Arty hardly moved as Marie and Peter entered the garden, apart from a raised head and a lethargic tail wag. They were getting used to the quieter life of retirement. Having found a cool, shady spot in which to sprawl, they saw no reason to move once they had recognised members of their extended pack.

Freya emerged with the rest of the food and crockery just a few minutes later. They ate their meal in the cooling evening breeze as Aston regaled his mother with all the news from the weekend. So much had happened in such a short space of time, even Freya wouldn't have known where to start.

"David and I found the boundary to Heimdall's land, which is really Erik's land, and we had a council of war, but I can't tell you about that. Then today we travelled back in time and met Rollo. He's going to teach me how to be a Viking and enlist me in the Great Army."

"Sounds like you'll be doing a lot more time travelling if you're to be part of the Great Viking Army," Peter said with a smile.

Marie looked at her mother questioningly.

"Rollo is part of the living history experience at Jorvik," Freya explained. "He was really very good with Aston and well informed on the finds from Coppergate. He told us Jorvik is running a children's camp in August. Aston's eager to go, but I've explained the decision is yours."

"Sounds interesting. Have you got the details and contact number?"

Before Freya could respond, Aston said, "I'll get them," and ran into the house. He quickly returned with the leaflet. Marie read it as he clung to her arm, excitement bubbling up. She passed the leaflet to Peter, but it was to Aston she spoke.

"Yes, you can go. It says we can book online. Is the computer set up, Mum?"

"Yes. David and Aston got it up and running last night. But finish your meal first. You too, Aston. Every great army must march on its stomach." She tried looking stern, but her eyes twinkled.

Peter waved the leaflet, saying, "These events fill up really quickly. It may be better to ignore the online application and telephone Rollo direct. It would, I think, be better if your mum does it, Marie. He'll remember her and Aston from today, and it may help secure his place. Never ignore a good contact." He handed the leaflet to Freya, who said firmly,

"Right. Tea first, then I'll phone."

As she finished off the last of her salad, she glanced up. Aston, Marie and Peter were all sitting straight-backed, arms folded, with empty plates in front of them. She held up her hands, palms out, in surrender.

"OK. I'm going to make the call. Give me a few minutes."

Aston went to follow her, but Marie held him back.

"Give your Nan some space. You won't have long to wait."

When Freya returned it wasn't with the news they were expecting,

"I'm afraid Rollo wasn't available, but I explained that I was ringing to confirm acceptance of his invitation for Aston to attend the Children's Re-enactors Camp. I've left my contact details and asked the lady to pass them on to Rollo."

Aston's disappointment was palpable, and Freya felt like she had let him down. She directed the rest of the information directly to Aston

"In the meantime, the lady advised that we should fill out the online form with all your details, to make sure you are in the system."

Marie stood up,

"Well, there's no time like the present. Let's try out the new computer and get it done."

As Aston and Marie vanished inside the cottage, Freya refreshed Peter's drink and topped up her own. Taking advantage of Aston's absence, she raised the subject of Daniel.

"I believe I owe you my thanks for defending my honour and sanity. Aston let it slip that Daniel had visited Marie. Thank you." She raised her glass.

"No need for thanks," Pater replied. "I only spoke the truth. He hasn't got a leg to stand on. Major Hodson wasn't too happy to learn of his accusations either. You've got nothing to worry about."

"Major Hodson? Has Daniel been harassing him too?" Freya was shocked. "I don't understand what has got into him."

"It was me who informed the major," Peter reassured her. "I thought he should be aware of it since it calls into question the competence of the British army to train and allocate handlers. He's confronted Daniel and his solicitor and left them in no doubt of your mental competence in general and ability to handle the wolves. The case has been dropped."

"Thank God for that! And thank God for the major too! No doubt he was more concerned with protecting the army rather than me, but it sounds like his intervention has been invaluable. Now all I need to think about is how to get to the bottom of Daniel's behaviour. Something is broken and I have to find a way of fixing it."

"You should leave Daniel to stew in his own juice," Marrie said, returning with Aston. "Whatever problem he has is of his own making."

Freya changed the subject, turning to Aston.

"So, are you all sorted?"

"Yeah! Mum filled the form out and they sent an instant reply to confirm my place. They'll send all the details shortly." He beamed, then flung himself around Freya's neck. "I love you, Nan. You're the best!"

It was exactly what she needed. She held him close as unbidden tears overflowed from her eyes.

"I love you too. You're my treasure beyond measure."

Then, releasing him, she excused herself quickly. "I'm so pleased you're sorted. I'm just going to get the presents we bought

64

for your mum and Rose." She hurried away, soon returning with the gifts. Handing the gift bags to Marie, she explained, "One is a silver necklace depicting Yggdrasil, the Viking tree of life. The other is a bracelet of amber beads, a replica of the finds discovered at the Coppergate dig. You and Rose can decide who has which one."

"I'm going to be very selfish and make the decision," Marie announced, rummaging in the bags to locate the boxed necklace. "Rose can have the bracelet. I'll wear the tree in honour of the Sentinel, the tree that changed our lives."

"Good choice," Peter approved, as he fastened it around her neck.

The summer evening was moving on, and a cooling breeze blew across the river. The wolves began to stir. Freya led them inside the garage to feed them and bed them down for the night. When she returned, she found Marie had cleared the table and was just finishing off the washing up.

"We'll get out of your hair now, Mum," she said, putting the last glass back on the shelf. "But I'm working on Tuesday, so could you have Aston for me?"

"Of course. I'll have my boy anytime. Let me know what time you'll drop him off."

"I'll call you," Marie promised, giving her mother a hug.

Thirty minutes later, having waved them off, Freya was ready to sink, exhausted, into her bed. Once more, across time and space, and perhaps from an alternative consciousness, dreams came.

11

Freya's Second Dream

Erik was leading his ships home in convoy, just as he had when they had set out. Travelling north, hugging the Danish coast, they only had to navigate the headland now before turning west on the strait for home. Then he would hand over the helm to Bjorn.

He clapped his son about the shoulders.

"You have made me proud. You left as a boy but will be returning as man and will know that you have brought me and your mother honour."

"I was already a man, Father," Bjorn laughed. "You just never noticed it."

Also laughing, Erik turned his attention to his men.

"Feasting tonight and whatever else takes your fancy. Not long now, men."

A cheer went up as they rowed with renewed strength.

From high in the rigging came a warning shout.

"Sails raised, heading west along the Joterlandshaff. Two warships, red sails showing Odin's Eye and Thor's Mjollnir."

Erik shouted commands. "Give the signal for my captains to join me." Then, to his crew, "Man the oars at half pace."

Swinging from ship to ship, Roar and Knud were soon beside him. Their own lookouts had given them the same warning.

"Warships! I would be happier if there were more than two, then they would undoubtedly sail on out to sea and away to Irland. Two makes me think they are foraging for supplies." Roar was the first to speak. Bjorn responded, emotion and panic giving an edge to his voice.

"If they are foraging off the coast, our homes and families are in danger. Why do we dawdle when we can chase them down? Three against two are good odds."

Many murmured their approval of Bjorn's plan, but Erik laid a steadying hand on his shoulder.

"They are already too close to home for us to reach them in time to be of any help. The best we could do is act as decoys. They

will know there will be little to find in the villages, and they may be tempted to turn away with the prospect of raiding three trading ships heading straight towards them."

"Foolishness! What good will it do our families if we openly invite these ships to take the supplies we have spent weeks gathering?" demanded Knud. "We will be condemning them to death by starvation. Divide the cargo of one ship between the other two and use the empty ship as bait."

Erik shook his head.

"It will take too long to transfer the cargo, and one ship with a crew made up of farmers and traders would be no match for the crews of two warships. I will not lead my men to certain death."

"We are wasting time with this debate." Bjorn was losing patience. "I say we all go now."

Screwing up his eyes, Erik shouted up to the lookout high in the rigging. "What are the ships doing?"

"Sailing straight ahead towards the open sea," came the reply.

"Then we sail on. My brothers, return to your ships with my thanks for your counsel."

Bjorn was at the helm as they approached home. The red-sailed warships had long since vanished around the headland into the open sea. At the village, no welcoming party was gathered to greet the three returning ships, only a silence that was palpable.

"Where is everyone?" Bjorn's voice was barely a whisper.

"It's likely they have taken refuge in the forest, as afraid as we were of the warships," Erik reassured his son. "Let's go seek them and give them the good news that they are safe and will be fed well enough until the spring."

Nevertheless, he gave orders for the cargo to be kept on the ships and left a guard to keep watch, as the rest of the men made their way into the village.

The devastation met them without mercy. The bodies of women and children had been left where they had met their death, mostly clustered around the homes that should have been a place of safety. The cries of the returning men as they ran to find their loved ones brought the silent village back to life, but it was a life that would never be the same again.

Erik found Astrid face down in a drying pool of blood just inside their home. His cry was heartrending.

"No! You cannot leave me!"

Kneeling, he pulled her into his arms, burying his face in her gore-stained hair.

"Astrid! You are my heart. I cannot live without you. Come back to me, my love."

But she could never come back. The knife she had used to cut her own throat rather than be violated was still clutched in her stiffened hand.

Hearing his father's cries, Bjorn came running, pausing just before he reached the doorway to take in the scene. Then he stumbled to his father's side, tears both blinding and choking him.

"Hel will not take her. She died with a weapon in her hand, fighting the only way she could." Erik pointed to the knife, knowing it would give comfort to Bjorn. "We will prepare her for the Valkyrie, but first we have to find the children."

As he laid Astrid gently down, a tiny, ghostlike whisper, "Fader!" came to him. Bjorn heard it also, and his keener eyesight spotted the tiny figure lying so close he could not fathom how they had not noticed it before.

"Freyja, Father! Freyja lives. She is here!"

The tiny child had been lying face down, clearly beneath her mother's body, which had hidden her from their view. Bjorn turned her gently over as he checked her for any injuries but the only blood she bore was her mother's. She breathed, but she was as limp as a rag doll and despite the one word she had managed to utter, she was unresponsive.

"She is so cold. Chaff her hands and feet, Bjorn. I will fetch her a clean warm gown and a blanket."

As Erik searched for Freyja's clothes, he prayed to the goddess for whom she was named.

"Most powerful and beautiful of all goddesses, Freyja, you who gave us the gift of this child, I beg you to keep watch over her and guide her back to us from the darkness which holds her. I beg you also to claim my wife, Astrid, who honoured you in all things. Be merciful and send the Valkyrie to guide her soul to your hall of Sessrumnir, for she died a warrior. She will bring grace and honour to your hall. Goddess, you know I speak the truth."

Erik took a deep breath and wiped his arm across his face before carrying the clothes back to where Bjorn was doing his best to warm and comfort his baby sister. A shadow blocked the light from the doorway.

"Bring the living to the Thingstead. There is warmth, care and warm food. We will provide what is needed for the dead once the living are found and cared for."

The speaker did not wait for a reply, limping away to carry his message elsewhere, but Erik had recognised the voice of Gothi Skarde the Black. Suddenly he was angry, so very angry he could not contain it. Scooping Freyja up, he stalked out of the house and yelled,

"You did not pray hard enough for the gods' protection. You did not fight hard enough to keep our families safe. We trusted you. You are a failure, Gothi Skarde."

Gothi Skarde stopped and turned.

"I know, Erik, and to say I am sorry for it is not enough. It will never be enough."

The Gothi turned and limped away, leaning heavily upon a stick. He had never needed the aid of a stick before. He had never had a limp before.

"Fader!" Bjorn's call had an urgent edge to it.

Erik turned to see his son hauling a strange man out of the house.

"I found him lying in a corner. He is not yet dead."

Erik thrust Freya towards his son, who let the man drop.

"This is for me to deal with alone. Take Freyja to the Thingstead, then look for your eldest sister and brothers. I will find you when I have done what is needed with this." Erik kicked the prone figure, who emitted a groan.

As Bjorn sped away, Erik hauled the man to the edge of the village.

"That she-wolf stabbed me in the eye. I would have done her no harm. I only wanted to pleasure her."

Manhandled into consciousness, the raider, having found his voice, had condemned himself beyond redemption. Erik gripped him by his leather jerkin, looking him in the eye.

"Do not plead injustice to me. By the time I have finished with you, you will think of that stab in the eye as an act of mercy.

You will not die the death of a warrior, as she did. You will not enter Valhalla. Your death will not be quick, and it will not be merciful. You are fit only for carrion."

As a farmer Erik had butchered many an animal for their table. Using only his axe, and starting at the feet, he performed the butchering of the raider slowly and without remorse. He left the meat to be consumed by whatever wild animal came along. The head he took with him.

Blood-spattered and exhausted, he made his way back to the house. Kneeling beside Astrid, he brushed the hair from her cheek, placing the head of the raider beside her.

"You did well, my love. Rest now. You are avenged."

12

Protector of the Sentinel

Freya's pillow was wet with tears when she awoke. Still emotionally engaged with her dream, she struggled to shake off the traumatic visions as she reoriented herself to face the day ahead. Dull-headed and with a heavy heart, she pushed away the covers and went for her morning shower. Another busy day lay ahead.

Today was the day she was going to give the Sentinel her full protection and establish her rights as owner of the land. With the prospect of Val Carey and the children descending for their class visit tomorrow, she had commissioned a sign board to be placed beside the field where the Sentinel stood. It would give a brief history of the Sentinel and the Viking settlement which had stood on the land. More importantly, as far as Freya was concerned, it would make it clear no public access was permitted as the land was privately owned. It was due to be delivered and erected at ten o'clock.

David arrived to give moral support at nine-thirty. Freya went out to greet him as he got out of the car.

"Good morning. Are you ready for this?" she asked, as he bent to give her a kiss on the cheek.

"Good morning, Freya. I'm excited. Have you been losing sleep over it? You look tired."

"No, I'm fine. I hope it looks OK though and I've got the wording right. I agonised over that."

"Just tell me it doesn't say 'Trespassers Will be Eaten by Wolves or Shot' and it will be fine." David gave her a hug.

Freya laughed. "No, I haven't gone that far. Don't worry."

They watched as a wagon pulled into the layby, then walked across together, as two workmen wearing yellow, reflective jackets climbed out.

"Morning, missus," the elder of the two said. "William and Billy Parsons, to erect your sign. Where do you want it?"

"Good morning. I hope you'll bear with me because I'm not a hundred per cent sure. Somewhere prominent that can easily be seen by oncoming traffic and walkers, without causing an impediment, but not blocking my view from the window. But first, could I check the sign to make sure there are no problems with the text or frame?"

The man gave a grunt. "Aye. Billy, climb up and unwrap the sign for the missus to look at."

Billy did as he was asked, and Freya and David pored over the sign.

"I like the colours, Freya," David remarked. "The gold lettering on that deep red background looks very regal."

Freya was pleased with it too.

"It does look nice, doesn't it? We better check there are no errors on the text."

Carefully they perused the wording together.

PROTECTED SITE OF SIGNIFICANT HISTORICAL INTEREST

The Sentinel is an English oak, believed to be 1,000–1,500 years old. It stands on land that was once part of a Viking settlement, which, according to ancient historical records was known as Heimdall's Land.

It is now on private property with absolutely no admittance to the public.

Enjoy the view but please respect the site.

Contact: F. Fraser at Sentinel Cottage

"That looks grand, Freya. Just the right balance." David smiled with satisfaction.

"If you're happy, missus, where do you want it?" the workman asked again.

Freya looked about, took a few paces to the right, and suggested, "About here, I think. Can you just hold the sign up at the right height, and I'll check it from the window?"

There was another grunt from the workman, but he and Billy carried the sign to the place Freya had indicated, while she

72

retreated to the house, looking out of the window. With a bit of arm waving indicating further right, she was finally happy the sign was in the right place. She returned to the workmen to confirm it.

"Right. Billy put this sign back in the lorry, and we'll get those posts out. A cup of tea and bacon bap would go down well, missus, before we start to dig out the post holes."

David had other ideas.

"You can be digging out the post holes while the tea and baps are being prepared. What are the posts made from?"

"Norwegian spruce, and they're not light to work with, so we better get on with it."

William Parsons was obviously a little put out. David laughed and clapped him on the shoulder.

"Good chap, that's the ticket. Tea and bacon baps will be with you shortly."

Freya had already gone back to the cottage to prepare the workers' breakfast, and now David followed suit. He was impressed that Freya had chosen to use Norwegian spruce for the posts. It was, he considered, a nice nod to the Norse connection with the land.

The men did an excellent job. The board was not only attached to the posts but was expertly recessed into them for extra strength and stability. Freya was thrilled and by the time David left, he was happy to see she seemed to have shaken off the tiredness and anxiety of the morning.

But had she?

13

Aston

Freya was excellent at pushing her concerns to one side so she could deal with what was required of her in the present. As she spent the rest of her day in peace and solitude with Fen and Arty as her only companions, she gave a lot of thought to the events of the weekend. So much had happened. She remembered little of her first dream, just fleeting images and snatches of conversations. But last night's dream had been graphic. It had been like watching a well-made film, so intense it sucked you into the story and emotions of the characters. It had sucked her into the life of Erik.

She gave Erik a lot of thought. Aston spoke of Erik a lot in connection with the Sentinel. Where had he found the name? What had made him knit together the details he thought were real? Was Erik real or had she simply overloaded on Viking history and absorbed Aston's imagined character into her own subconscious? She didn't know, but she was determined to find out whatever she could. In the warmth of the day, she sat in the shade, the wolves by her side, and wrote out all she could remember of her dreams.

Tuesday morning arrived without any dreams to add to Freya's dream diary. It did, however, bring with it a thunderstorm of almost biblical proportions. The lightning flashed and cracked almost incessantly, while the thunder rolled and rumbled so loudly it was like being bombarded by explosions. The wolves howled and paced, whether in fear or with wild excitement, Freya wasn't sure. It was only five a.m., so she used a large blanket to cover their pen, hoping the darkness would sooth them. But there was nothing she could do to block out the noise of the storm.

Gradually the howling ceased as the storm slowly abated. Her greatest fear – that the Sentinel would be damaged by the lightning – proved ungrounded. When she went out to check, carrying her second coffee of the morning, the Sentinel not only stood proud, but seemed to stretch out to welcome the much-needed moisture. She looked at the lowering steel-grey sky with its black rolling clouds.

"There's plenty more to come," she said to the tree. "You can drink your fill."

She scarcely had time to shower and dress before Marie arrived with Aston.

"Sorry we're early. I'm hoping to dodge the next downpour. The new sign looks amazing," Marie enthused. "My only criticism is that you should have said 'Trespassers Will be Eaten by Wolves'."

"Now, that's what David was most happy to see I'd avoided."

They both laughed. Then Marie glanced at her watch.

"I've got a bit of time for breakfast if there's any on offer. Aston hasn't had any either." She gave a cheeky grin.

"I should change the name of the cottage to the Sentinel Tea Rooms. I had to feed the workmen who did the sign yesterday." Freya let out an exaggerated sigh as she began to prepare a decent breakfast for them all. Really, she was rather pleased to have their company for the morning meal. It was a touch of normality after what had been a very unsettling weekend.

Once Marie had left for work, Freya and Aston donned their coats and wellies to take Fen and Arty for their exercise. The heavy downpour must have washed away some of their scent, for the wolves occupied themselves rolling and squirming in the mud at every opportunity. Freya was as amused as Aston by their antics. At least she was until they got back home, when she realised her beautiful grey wolves were now camouflaged in thick black mud and red clay, and it was her job to clean them. She frowned at the wolves as though they were mischievous children.

"Well, you've had a fine old time. But where am I supposed to start to get you both clean?"

The wolves responded by wagging their tails and rubbing their muddy bodies on her legs. She pushed them away gently.

"Enough. Boys. At rest, Private Fen and Private Arty."

The two wolves sat obediently, and some order might have been attained if Aston had not flung himself down to hug Arty.

"You need a bath, Arty. You're blacker than a coalman." As he looked up at Freya, she saw a lump of red clay clung to his hair and his own face was streaked with mud.

"You'll be in the bath with them at this rate, young man! Take your coat and wellies off by the sink and get a quick wash. I'll have to let the boys dry off a bit and hope I can brush off most of the mud later."

She rummaged in a cupboard beside the wolf pen as she spoke, pulling out two large, all-weather dog coats with legs, which she threw to one side.

"It's a bit late for those now, but I'm sure there should be two drying wraps here, to absorb most of the wet and mud. Ah, here they are."

As Aston washed, she wrapped the two wolves in warm, absorbent towelling coats and set about feeding them, before putting them back in their pen.

"Time to pay for your sins," she told them, as she and Aston left them to dry out. "We'll be back in a bit."

The storm returned not long after, quickly followed by the shrill tone of the telephone.

"Ms Fraser." Miss Carey's voice travelled down the line. "I'm sorry to let you down at such short notice. But the parents are a bit nervous about the children being out in the storm. I'm afraid we won't make it this morning."

Silently, Freya raised her hands in a prayer of thanks, but then she said, "Don't worry, Miss Carey, I understand completely. The weather is appalling."

"I hope it's all right with you," Miss Carey continued, "but I've suggested to parents that they may like to drive by at some point over the holidays, to give their children the opportunity to see the Sentinel. Naturally you won't be expected to host them in any way."

"That's fine, Miss Carey. Thank you for letting me know. Bye."

Freya hung up the phone with a smug smile, then told Aston the news. He didn't seem bothered.

"I've already told them there are photographs of the Sentinel online, so there's no need to come. It will give us more time to bath and groom Fen and Arty, anyway."

Freya was surprised

"I thought you wanted them to come?"

Aston gave a shrug but wouldn't look up. Freya sat down beside him.

"OK, spill the beans. What's been going on? Are you being bullied?"

Aston, his knees pulled up to his chest, shrugged again, but remained silent. Freya's concern stepped up a pace. She reached for his hand.

"Come on, love. Whatever it is, we can sort it out. But I need to know what's been happening first. I promise you, I will sort it out."

Aston remained reluctant to say anything. Knowing that continuing to badger him would only make him more reluctant to speak, Freya stood up.

"OK. Let's leave it for now and do something nice. But give it some thought. If you don't trust me, don't tell me. But I hope you do trust me. And when you want to tell me, I'll be ready to listen."

The rain was still falling in torrents, spilling large, heavy drops from the heavens. Thunder drops, Freya called them, though for now the thunder was silent and the lightning remained at bay. She began to set up the computer and placed a good selection of snacks on the table.

"Come on. We'll work on your assignment. We can download all the photographs from the Jorvik Viking Centre

Aston got up and, walking away from the table, went to stand by the lounge window, which overlooked the road and the Sentinel. With his back to Freya, he said,

"There's no point in working on the assignment. Miss Carey says I can't submit it anyway."

Freya was frozen for a second or two. Then, struggling to contain the shock and anger she felt at Aston's words, she managed to keep her voice calm and even toned.

"What did Miss Carey say exactly? Can you remember?"

"She said I'd been getting too much help and that put the rest of the class at a disadvantage, so I couldn't submit it. She thinks getting help is cheating."

"Does she really? I wonder why she suggested that I help and support you to do the assignment in the first place, if she thinks it's cheating. Anyway, let's ignore Miss Carey for now. What do you think? What do you want to do?"

"What do you mean?" Aston asked uncertainly.

"Well, have you enjoyed working on the assignment and learning about the Sentinel and the Viking settlement? Or have you been bored and hated it?"

"I haven't been bored. It's been really cool and exciting."

"Good. That's what I wanted to know. So, ignoring Miss Carey and thinking only about what you would like, would you like to go on and see what else there is to discover? Or would you rather lose all that work you've done and bin it? Remember, the only person who matters here is you."

"Can I think about it? I don't want to bin it."

"Of course. You can give it as much thought as you like. But think about what is right for you. Now, come and help me eat some of these snacks."

Before Aston could move, they heard a car pulling into the driveway. Thinking it was likely the parents of one of the children, parking in the wrong place, Freya went to the door. A young man with long hair tied back in a ponytail got out, accompanied by another person, bedecked in a long cloak.

"It's Rollo!" Aston ran past her before she could stop him, greeting Rollo like a long-lost friend.

After Aston's upsetting revelations, Rollo could not have been more welcome. Despite only a brief acquaintance, Freya had a good feeling that the re-enactor could help Aston more than she could at this point. She called out to him.

"What a pleasant surprise! Come in out of the rain."

Once they were all inside, Rollo's companion removed the cloak to reveal a stunningly beautiful young woman, with hair the palest shade of blonde, bound in long Heidi-style plaits. As Rollo introduced her as his wife, she took Freya's hand in greeting, holding her gaze. Freya found she could not look away. The woman's eyes were of the palest blue, so pale they gave off more than a hint of a silvery-grey tinge.

"You have the soul of a protector, all will be well in your hands. My name is, Mànésdottor which means Daughter of the Moon. I am pleased to meet you, please call me Màné." she said warmly to Freya. The words broke the spell.

Freya took her cloak and busied herself making her unexpected guests welcome before she noticed that Aston was clutching a brown paper parcel.

"Our apologies for calling unannounced, but we are busy with the preparations for next week's children's camp," Rollo said. "We want the children to come prepared in costume, so we are making our deliveries. I hope it fits you, Aston."

"It will fit," Màné assured them.

"Try it on, Aston," urged Freya. "I can't wait to see you all costumed up."

She expected Aston to vanish into his room to change, but unabashed he performed the task there and then, accepting Rollo's help with unfamiliar fastenings. Rollo encouraged him, giving him the names of each item of clothing.

"You will need to practise dressing, so you can do it for yourself," he said. "It's not difficult once you get used to the points and lacings."

Meanwhile, to give Aston some privacy, Màné had discreetly wandered away, feigning interest in the computer. She caught Freya's eye.

"May I?" she enquired.

"Of course," Freya said. "It's Aston's school assignment, outlining what he's discovered about the history of the Sentinel. He's a bit undecided about it."

Soon Aston was kitted out and being celebrated by Freya. Màné, meanwhile, was absorbed by the contents of the computer and looked up only when Rollo called her.

"I'm so sorry," she said. "You look every inch the son of a Viking, Aston. Superb. And this is a fantastic piece of work. You should take a look, Rollo."

Rolo checked the time.

"We should be going, Màné. There's a lot for us to get through today."

But Màné would not be deterred.

"A few more minutes won't hurt. And I'm sure Aston would be eager to have your opinion. It's really very, very good."

Resigned, Rollo went to the computer, with Aston sticking to his side like a limpet. In no time he was as absorbed in Aston's work as Màné had been. Aston told him all about what both Miss Carey and Freya had said. Rollo tried to give a balanced, independent assessment.

"First, I have a question for you to answer honestly, Aston. How much of this work is your own, and how much help have you had?"

Aston didn't hesitate.

"I got most of it from the internet. And Nan has helped. She found the records of the land and boundary maps. David helped me when we walked the boundary and tried mapping it out. But I've put it all into the computer for the assignment myself."

"That's great. So no excessive help then, and no help with putting it all together. Very well done to you, Aston. Now, I can see why Miss Carey would be worrying about the chances of the other children. It is far too good to be a simple school assignment, but she cannot stop you submitting your assignment or from being fairly assessed. That's discrimination and not only is it wrong, but it is also against the law."

"That's what I was thinking," Freya put in. "I'm going to lodge a strong complaint. Miss Carey's decision has upset him so much."

"Quite right too," Màné agreed. Seeing that Rollo had more to say but was hesitant to put his thoughts into words, she went to stand beside him, laying her hand on his shoulder. This simple act seemed to bring him to a decision.

"I'm wondering, Aston, would you mind if I shared your file with a friend who may be able to help you decide what you need to do next?"

Aston looked at Freya before replying. "I don't mind. But won't Miss Carey say I'm cheating if I get more help?"

"I promise, nothing will be added or taken away from your own writing, and it won't be shared with anyone else in any form. But I do think his advice could help you."

Once more Aston looked at Freya.

"What do you think, Nan?"

"As long as it's shared safely and not indiscriminately, I can't see a problem," she said. "It's your work though, so it's your decision."

"OK." Aston nodded at Rollo.

With a few clicks Rollo added a copyright notice identifying Aston as the legal author and owner of the material, before sending the file to his own email address.

"I've sent it to myself for now, but I'll send it on to my friend tonight with an explanation. Aston is the legal owner of the copyright. I hope that's OK." Then he stood up. "Now we really will have to go. I'm sorry we stole so much of your day. If I'm not in touch before, I'll see you next week at camp, young warrior."

Thanks and farewells were exchanged, and once Rollo and Màné had departed, Aston spent the rest of the afternoon working on his assignment, still in his costume. Miss Carey's objections were forgotten.

The storm began to move away, and the sun struggled through the lingering clouds. Traffic increased on the road and Freya noticed three or four cars stop briefly in the layby, although nobody got out. Were these some of the more "dedicated" parents who felt obliged to bring their child to visit the Sentinel, perhaps taking any photographs discreetly through a wound-down window before driving off again, duty done? That suited her perfectly.

After being concerned that Aston would abandon his assignment, Freya now had to use all her powers of persuasion to drag him away from it.

"I wonder what Vikings ate?" she asked nonchalantly.

Aston looked up, a puzzled frown on his face. It was obviously something he had given little previous thought to. After a few minutes he said,

"I think they ate a lot of meat and got drunk."

"Did they? That must have been very boring after a while. Didn't they eat bread or cake?"

Aston shrugged, then clicked on Google Search.

"I'll look."

In no time he was reading off a list of favourite Viking foods, alighting on one in particular.

"Hogsnott! Can we make Hogsnott, Nan?"

"Dear lord, Aston, I don't think so. I feel quite ill! What on earth is Hogsnott? On second thoughts, don't tell me. I don't think I want to know."

Aston was almost doubled over with giggles.

"It's not what you're thinking, Nan. It's just hog snouts, boiled and then pressed into a pâté for eating on bread." He was reading from the recipe as he spoke.

Freya still found it unappealing.

81

"The nearest I have in the fridge is bacon. That's all I have in the hog line. So, we can make one of the bread recipes and have it with bacon and honey. What do you think? Print off the recipes and we'll have a go."

"I can take some of the bread to Rollo, can't I, Nan?"

"That's a good idea. If we make a good job of it, we can pop one in the freezer for you to take to him next week."

On Freya's advice, Aston changed out of his costume and folded it neatly back into the parcel to make sure it stayed clean. Soon they were poring over the bread recipe in the kitchen. Freya collected the ingredients and Aston weighed them out. Soon the table was filled with a variety of bowls holding:

Three cups of whole-wheat flour,

Two cups of all-purpose flour

One teaspoon of baking soda, plus one of salt

Two cups of water

Three-quarters of a cup of rolled oats, plus another one-third of a cup of the same for sprinkling on top

Freya checked the recipe again.

"Right, now we have to put all of this into a bowl, add the water and give it a good stir."

"I'll do it, Nan," Aston said enthusiastically.

"Great. Stir until you can't stir anymore, then I'll try to stir a bit more. The mixture must be stiff. Then we have to knead it."

"What does that mean?"

"Kneading? It means we need to push, pull and thump the dough to make sure all the flour is really well mixed in."

Between them the bread was soon in the oven to be baked for an hour.

Aston stacked the dishwasher, while Freya used the baking time to prepare a lasagne for tea. She was sure Marie would be happy to have a cooked meal ready and waiting for her when she arrived from work to collect Aston. And they had so much to tell her over the meal.

14

Dreamscapes

Much later, Freya sat alone, reflecting not just on the day that was coming to an end, but on the twists and turns her life had taken over the past few months. She was a changed woman. The downtrodden, soulless zombie whose one focus was to get through each day with her mundane tasks completed had been reborn. Now she had interests, she made plans. She had a social network and no longer lived her life in isolation. The lottery win was not at the root of this change, though it had facilitated it. The root was the place, the Sentinel, the homestead, Fen and Arty, and the people who had somehow gathered around her to support her.

On the face of it, all this looked like it had occurred randomly, by chance, by luck, by coincidence. But deep within her soul, Freya sensed nothing was random about her settling at Sentinel Cottage. It was meant to be. She had been called home for a purpose. And that purpose involved Marie, Aston, David, Peter, Rollo and Màné. Of this she was convinced.

That night the dreams returned.

"Fader!"

Erik was making his way to the Thingstead when he heard Bjorn's call. He turned, watching as his eldest son hurried up to him.

"Gorm is safe. He had led the animals to safety in the forest with others. They have returned to the Thingstead. I cannot find Thurid or Ulf. There is talk that many were taken as slaves."

Images of Thurid's blossoming beauty and Ulf's earnest face as he had made his plea to be taken on the voyage flashed before Erik's eyes. He covered his face with his hands as though attempting to hide the images and he breathed deeply. The he asked urgently,

"Where have you looked?"

"The village has been well searched. There was some fighting around the Thingstead. Gothi Njal and Gothi Birger were

killed. Gothi Skarde was injured and left for dead. He can tell us nothing of what followed afterwards." Despite his fear and emotional turmoil, Bjorn did his best to report what he knew accurately and concisely.

"Did any of the raiders survive?" Erik felt a pang of regret that he had not questioned the raider who had violated his wife before killing him.

Bjorn shook his head.

"Not all of them got away, but none were found alive. Gothi Skarde has had their corpses hung from the trees."

"We will search on the river path. Neither Ulf nor Thurid would go quietly. If they were being forced down to the ships, we may find signs of them there."

Erik and Bjorn made their way down the muddy slope towards the water's edge, with care, searching ahead and from side to side as they went for any sign of Ulf or Thurid.

Suddenly Erik broke into a run, heading to the thick mud of the water's edge, crying "Ulf!"

Bjorn was not far behind.

Ulf lay face down in the mud, a spear in his young back, but he had not died alone. Beside him lay one of the raiders, a piece of blue ribbon clutched in his hand. Embedded in the back of his skull was Ulf's axe. A girl's shoe poked out of the mud.

As Erik pulled the spear from Ulf's back and his son's axe from the raider's skull, Bjorn picked up the shoe and groped about in the mud for any sign of his sister. There was none.

Kneeling in the mud, Erik cradled his son to his chest, crooning to him.

"I should have taken you with me. I should have taken you all with me. Forgive me, my son. I was a fool to leave you with only the old and weak to protect you."

Bjorn was angry.

"We should not have delayed. If we had come as soon as we saw the warships, we could have been here."

Erik shook his head.

"It was already too late. The attack must have happened before we saw the sails being raised. But we will find them, I swear to you, Bjorn. We will hunt them down and we will bring Thurid back to us. I swear this by all the gods."

84

Many men had been carrying out their own searches in the mud and river weeds. Now, the blowing of a horn called them to return to the Thingstead. One or two, like Erik, carried the body of a loved one. A few hauled the remains of a raider left behind. One raider was still alive. He would be taken to Gothi Skarde to be questioned before being hanged.

Erik and Bjorn carried the body of Ulf to lie beside Astrid. It was a hurried act for they needed to get to the Thingstead to hear what the raider had to say. Questions must be raised, and decisions taken.

The Thingstead was dimly lit, smoky, and smelled of death, vomit and despair. Women wailed while children cried for their mothers' arms. Erik found Freyja beside the fire, in the arms of Astrid's ageing grandmother, Revna. Erik knelt beside her.

"How goes the child, Grandmother?"

Ravna opened her cloak. Freyja looked lifeless, limp, with the blue tinge of death around her eyes and mouth.

"She lives, but it is not good, Erik. This child suffered everything that my granddaughter suffered." She saw the look in Erik's eyes and was quick to amend her words. "Oh, not physically. Do not fear the worst. But she lay beneath her mother throughout her trials. She felt Astrid's fear, her anger, her humiliation, and her lifeblood flowing from her body. She felt her last breath and feels it still. It is not good."

Overwhelmed, Erik was lost for words. He reached out and touched the little one's cheek.

"What do we need to do? Will she get well? Or is she condemned to this living death? Grandmother, help me please, for I am lost." He fought back the tears and heartbreak that threatened to unman him.

"Part of her lies on the plain of death with her mother. We must summon the Seidr to seek her and bring her back. Only the Seidr can help." Ravna offered her opinion thoughtfully, with a touch of fear.

Erik was reluctant.

"Is there no other way?"

The Seidr were powerful magicians, who could travel between worlds. Sometimes they could give life. More often, they took it.

85

Ravna and Erik had lowered their voices and now spoke in whispers.

"I have thought on it all day. This child is a gift from the goddess Freyja. Astrid always believed it was so. The goddess was also a Seidr. Would she not share her skills to rescue and return her gift? I can see no other way." Ravna held Erik's gaze until he responded.

"If that is our only option, then we take it. I will pay any price asked if my Freyja can be returned to us. Do you know how to summon the Seidr, Grandmother?"

Ravna, nodded. "I do."

Erik placed his hands on the old woman's shoulders.

"Then do it. But make sure it is known the debt is mine and mine alone. No other will pay the price." He knew the Seidr never gave their services except at a high price, often asking a life for a life.

Some time later, as dusk was falling, villagers gathered in their homes to prepare their dead for the funeral pyres. Some would make the journey under the sacred hill, to place their dead among the ancestors.

In Erik's house, Ravna and one of the village women prepared Astrid and Ulf for their journey, either to Odin's hall of Valhalla or to Freyja's hall of Sessrumnir, where they would be honoured as warriors. Erik handed Ravna a silver torc.

"Put this on her. I bought it as a gift for her. She should wear it and carry my love with her."

Silently, Ravna placed the torc around the neck of her granddaughter.

Bjorn and Gorm handed her two arm rings, the reward of warriors who had fought valiantly.

"We had Arne the blacksmith fashion these. One for our mother, the other for our brother."

Ravna took the rings and placed them on the right arms of Astrid and Ulf, then Erik and Bjorn placed their bodies on wattle biers for transport to the pyre. Erik kissed his wife and son for the last time, as Ravna placed sacred herbs into their hands and crowns of greenery from the forest upon their heads.

"You have served them well, Grandmother. My wife looks like a queen. This saffron dress was her favourite. My brave Ulf is *every inch the warrior. Gorm, you may have the honour of placing their weapons beside them, then all is ready."*

Struggling to act much older than his nine years, Gorm carefully placed Astrid's knife in her hand and Ulf's axe in his. He bowed solemnly as he did so, paying his own respects and saying his personal goodbye to his mother and brother.

"Fetch me the child."

The family all turned at the sound of the unfamiliar voice. From the darkest recesses of the room a cloaked figure walked towards them. The Seidr had arrived.

Erik signalled for his family to leave, but the Seidr said, *"You all must stay. The child is bound to all of you. We must break the bonds with the dead and pull her back into the bonds of her living family."* She aimed her next words directly to Erik.

"Go now and do my bidding. Fetch the child to me."

With Erik gone, the Seidr began her task, while the waiting family looked on. They drew closer to one another for comfort, as the woman bent and stretched and twirled in every darkened corner of the room, muttering incantations, and sending the smoke from burning herbs towards the rafters. After some time, she announced with satisfaction,

"All is cleansed. The Husvaettir are placated. They give their blessing to our task. The Illvatte and Nisse are bound and banished and will cause no trouble. Now you must form a circle, an arm's length apart. Do it quickly so a place can be prepared for the child."

It was not much of a circle, made up of just Gorm, Bjorn and Ravna. The Seidr went from one to the other, placing their hands gently together, before circling their wrists with a pointed finger.

"These are the ties that bind, each to the other."

By the time she had finished, to their amazement, a strong cord had been woven, forming a cats-cradle, between the three. Though Gorm and Bjorn instinctively tried to free themselves, the cords were unbreakable.

Once more the Seidr went from one to the other, aiding them to drink from a clay cup, as she whispered, *"Be seated."* Now all were seated before the fire, the bindings forming a soft receptacle, almost crib-like, between them.

Erik announced his return by almost stumbling through the doorway, Freyja in his arms. The tiny child was almost lost to view, wrapped snugly in a fur blanket. The Seidr did not look round.

"Place the child among the bindings of her kin and take your place in the circle."

Though filled with fear and trepidation, though his mind spun with questions, Erik obeyed, without one of those questions being given a voice. This was what he had asked for. He had agreed to the Seidr being summoned. Now he had to obey her every command.

She spoke to him again.

"Erik the trader, you are the father of this child who floats between the worlds. Are you prepared to travel into the darkness, wrestle with the spirits, and join your force with the goddess Freyja against the goddess Hel, to restore your child to the living realm?"

Erik did not hesitate.

"I will do whatever I must, and I will not fail."

The Seidr nodded her approval, and bound Erik's hands, just she had bound the others.

"These are the ties that bind. Let them be joined, each to the other and all to the child."

Erik watched as invisible bonds became visible, tangible cords, which writhed like serpents between members of his family and encased his daughter in a cocoon of blue thread.

The Seidr moved towards the resting corpses of Astrid and Ulf, and performed a similar act of magic. Waving her hands over both, she muttered incantations, before saying,

"These are the bonds which must be severed, and every trace removed from the web."

A red cord writhed and weaved its way from the dead to the child, and eventually to Erik.

The Seidr returned to Erik.

"All is now prepared. You must hold tight to the cords that bind, and find the red cords, which you must sever. You must remove every trace, in order to bring your child back. Erik the trader, stand and face the flames of Hel. Are you ready for your journey?"

Erik stood as the flames in the fire grew higher and crackled ominously.

"I am ready," he said firmly.

88

"Then I send you forward."

Without further warning, the Seidr gave Erik a mighty push, sending him into the crackling flames to be engulfed by utter darkness. From out of the darkness the face of the Seidr hovered, all knowing, all seeing, all knowledgeable.

Freya sat up in bed, suddenly fully awake. The face of the Seidr still hovered before her eyes. It was Màné.

It was not the dream, but the image of Màné that played on Freya's mind for the rest of the day. She spent it alone, walking with the wolves. She was not usually given to fanciful notions, but she had felt a power emanating from the young woman that she could not deny, and it disturbed her. Perhaps she just had too much time to think, she reasoned, but she was not convinced by her own suggestion. It worried her. Was Màné a source of help or danger?

Over the next three nights the dreams continued with graphic intensity.

Erik lay on the floor of the dwelling, his daughter in his arms. Neither moved. Around him, Ravna, Bjorn and Gorm began to stir, as if waking from a dream. The binding cords were gone.

Outside, a drum beat and sounds of activity filtered through. Bjorn stood and staggered slightly as he walked to the door.

"It is time. We must go. The pyres are being prepared."

He tried rousing his father, but Erik's sleep was too deep to be penetrated, as was Freya's. Bjorn satisfied himself that it was only sleep. His father and sister were breathing normally.

"Gorm, you must help me with the pyre. Grandmother, keep trying to rouse father. He must attend."

"He will not be roused," came a voice from the darkness. "He will sleep until tomorrow and will remember nothing of this day. It is the price he pays for severing the bonds to save his daughter. Your sister will sleep until she awakes in a new land far away. She will be the founder of a line of guardians, who will protect the land from invaders for all time."

With these, her last words, the Seidr was gone. No one saw her leave, just as none had seen her arrive.

The funeral pyres burned bright as the villagers who remained feasted in honour of their dead. The absence of Erik did not go unnoticed. Both Roar and Knud faced Bjorn angrily.

"Where is your father, Bjorn? As head of the family, he should be here to honour our dead. Is he too drunk to do his duty?"

Bjorn was not intimidated by his uncles.

"In the absence of my mother, my father is doing what only a loving father could do. He is giving care and protection to my sister. She is too young and too sick to face this and cannot be left alone. I am acting for my father. Our dead are being shown all honour. Have I not acted as I should?"

Erik's brothers were chastened.

"Aye, you have done all that was needed. Forgive us. We had forgotten about little Freyja. But there are things to be settled, questions to be answered, and plans and preparations to be made for the future."

"My father has already made his decision. We will be sailing to search for those who have been enslaved. Any who wish to sail with us may do so, and any who wish passage to another land for a fresh start may also sail with us"

"When was this decided? We have not been consulted about this."

"My father and I settled it yesterday between ourselves, but there has been no time for anything else except preparing our dead. Let us get through this night with only our dead in our thoughts and in our hearts. Tomorrow, my father will speak to you, and to all the village. All can make their own decisions then. Come, drink with me as we wait for the Valkyrie to bear off the souls of those who fought so valiantly."

As his uncles, duly placated, clapped him on the back in acceptance, Bjorn hoped he had spoken the truth and that, on the morrow, his father would have recovered enough to do as he had promised.

The rising smoke from the pyres turned with time from black to grey and eventually to white, as the Valkyrie bore away the souls to Odin in Valhalla or to the goddess Freyja in Sessrumnir. Only a few of the very old or very young who had not died as warriors would find themselves in the hall of Hel.

In the dim light of dawn, Erik walked out of the dwelling to the sight of the smouldering pyres. He had been furious with Bjorn when he realised the boy had allowed him to sleep through the honouring of the dead. Ravna's explanation had placated him only a little. He should have stood by Astrid's side and given his blessing to Ulf, in full honour of their courage and their shared love. But he had cut those bonds by the command of the Seidr and had given up his right to claim the honour of keeping vigil over their journey into the other world. He had been harsh with Bjorn, and now he was sorry for it.

Slowly he made his way to the still-smouldering pyres of his wife and son, their remains now nothing but ash. The necklace he had given her lay blackened. Her knife was twisted and scorched, still too hot to handle. He let them lie, though he longed for the tangible touch of these personal and precious memories.

"Forgive me, Astrid. I was not a good husband to you. I think I am not a good father. Too often I let you down and I failed to protect you. We are going away, me and the children. Your mother also, I hope, though she says she will stay. I cannot leave her behind, defenceless and alone, so I will persuade her."

He paused to control the raw emotion of what he was feeling, the enormity of what he was planning to do. He gazed up at the smoke-stained clouds, just letting himself breathe, until he felt composed enough to go on.

"We cannot stay here. Thurid has been stolen by the raiders. I must look for her. Freyja is sick. The Seidr has said she will recover but not until she is in a new land far away from here. Given this chance, in time, she will do great things. It was said that she will be the founder of a line of guardians who will protect the land from invaders for all time. I must give her that chance."

A light breeze stirred the ashes and blew against his cheek. It felt like a caress against his rough, dry skin. He covered the spot with his own hand, as though placing it over Astrid's.

"There is one more thing I must tell you. I have spoken of this to no other, for I know I will be breaking our ancient customs. I need your blessing and approval for it. I ask your understanding. I am taking you and Ulf with me. I will carry your ashes and when we find a new land, I will place them in the ground beneath a sacred tree. Our new life will be built on this nur sidr, a new custom."

He turned to walk away, then abruptly turned round as though he had heard the calling of his name.

"I have to do it, Astrid. I cannot leave you and Ulf behind. I cannot live without you close to me."

"Erik!"

This time the voice was real. It belonged to his brother, Roar.

"Erik. We need to talk."

"Yes, I know, brother. There are many decisions and plans to be discussed. I am calling a meeting at the Thingstead. Come. We will arrange it together and collect Knud on the way. First, we will fetch Bjorn."

The scene changed. Time had elapsed.

The ships were sailing low in the water, the sails raised to harness the fair wind, blowing along the Jutland coastline. Roar was not a happy captain as he looked at the many faces that looked back at him. All wore bleak expressions as they huddled wherever they could find a space.

"My brother has miscalculated the capacity of his ships, I think. We could manage the extra passengers, or the extra cargo, but both together is going to prove a problem when we enter the open sea."

He had not realised he had spoken his thoughts out loud, so hearing a reply surprised him. It came from a man who had been leaning on the ship's rail.

"What else could he do? We have all suffered losses, either to death or to slavery. Women have been left widowed, children orphaned. There were not many wanting to stay behind. How could he choose who to leave? I thank the gods for your brother's generosity."

Roar sighed. He knew the man was right. Skellig Skelligson had been his neighbour for years as well as a regular member of his crew. He too had lost a son and daughter to the slave ships and had vowed his intent, like Erik, to hunt them down.

"Forgive me, Skellig. I spoke out of turn, without thinking. So many lives turned upside down, so many hopes resting on this voyage. The responsibility sits heavy on my shoulders."

Skellig shot a quick look around before replying in a conspiratorial tone, *"We could be in no better hands, captain. Don't tell him I said this, but your knowledge of the sea is even greater than Erik's."*

He winked, making Roar laugh.

The signal came from Erik's ship to turn westward, veering away from the Norse coastline and out into the North Sea and open water.

Roar returned his attention to the helm, glancing at the sky as he did so. There was nothing to indicate bad weather. The wind was fair, the sea calm, for which he thanked the gods. Despite Skellig's encouragement, Roar did not want to be put to the test with so many lives in his hands.

Knud followed his brothers westward. His ship was not as overburdened with passengers as Roar's, but nevertheless, he felt the responsibility just as Roar did. There had been no sacrifices this time to mark their voyage. It had been agreed that the animals should be divided to allow a food source (however scrawny they were) for those remaining behind and a start for those seeking a new life in a foreign land. Transporting them had fallen to Knud. With the sails raised and catching the wind, there was little need for rowing. He set his men to other tasks.

"I want those animals cleaned, fed and watered, in that order. They stink! Get to it."

Grumbling, his crew complied, hauling buckets of water from the sea and sluicing away the detritus the animals had produced.

They sailed on, making good speed, Knud at the helm, singing to himself.

Erik had not spared himself the responsibility of carrying passengers. Most of the village had decided it was time to leave and find safety elsewhere. Only the very old, the terminally sick and unclaimed orphans had remained behind, under the care and protection of the Gothi. Erik had his doubts just how much care and protection the Gothi could give, but there was nothing he could do to alter that. As he manned the helm towards Angleland, he turned to Bjorn.

"Check on the villagers and bring me back news of your sister and grandmother."

Bjorn obeyed without hesitation. He was soon back.

"Most are faring well enough, though two of the old widow women are sick with the motion of the ship. Grandmother is overseeing them and says she will do what she can. Freyja still sleeps."

Erik nodded.

"Only two are ill. That is good. Your grandmother will care well for them. Freyja will be well enough when we reach land. The Seidr promised."

"How long will that take?" Bjorn asked, out of curiosity more than anything else.

Erik was cautious in his reply.

"We are in the hands of the gods. But if this good weather keeps up, we should make land in another two days, maybe three." He handed the helm to Bjorn. "Here, get some experience of the helm in open sea. Feel for the difference in the currents."

Freya rolled over in her sleep, a small groan escaping her lips. Slowly she dragged herself from sleep. She felt nauseous and her tummy growled, gently but ominously. The call for the loo couldn't be ignored. She pushed herself to sit up, then quickly lay back down as a wave of vertigo sent the room spinning around her. It felt like her bed had turned into a canoe going down rapids. Groaning again, she gave in helplessly to whatever ailed her, concentrating only on her breathing as she waited for the nausea and vertigo to pass. Sleep and dreams claimed her once more.

A storm held the three ships in a maelstrom of rain, wind and pitching waves. The fearful cries of the helpless passengers mingled with the yelled orders of the captains as they struggled to maintain control of the helm.

"Man the oars! Maintain our position."

"Lash everything down, including the women and children."

"Mighty Thor, be not angry with us, but show us mercy."

"Save me from the monsters of the deep. Do not let me be cast into their angry realm."

"Do not lash me to the ship, lest it sink, and I cannot escape."

94

"Mighty Njord, ruler of the seas, protect us. If we have caused offence, forgive us."

The prayers and the pleas went on and on as the force of the storm increased, and the ships were battered by mighty waves.

The child, Freyja, awoke and began to scream. It was a bad omen, forcing Erik into a decision to make a sacrifice to the gods, Njord and Thor.

He called to his crew. "Increase the number of men on the oars. Relieve those in place."

The tired men who had been battling against the pull of the sea for some time were relieved, as there was a scramble to obey their captain's orders.

"We need to pull alongside Knud's ship. It will not be easy, but it must be done. Pull!"

Seeing what Erik intended, Roar followed suit. He was not going to be left out of any intended plans.

The manoeuvre was neither easy nor quick, calling on the combined skills of the captains and their oarsmen, but it was achieved,

"Maintain an oar's length between the ships," Erik commanded, as against all the odds he attempted to swing across on to Knud's ship.

Blinded by rain, buffeted by the wind, battered by the force of the waves, Erik thanked the gods for their mercy, as Knud and Roar reached to pull him aboard. He was not surprised to find Roar there before him. He quickly made them aware of what was needed.

"The fault is mine. I ignored the need for a sacrifice before we left, and I have made the gods angry. We will sacrifice one of my horses."

"We are all at fault, Erik. We made that decision jointly." Roar attempted to comfort his older brother.

"Now we will put it right and show Njord we honour him, but it won't be so simple to achieve," warned Knud. "The animals are wild with fear. I have hobbled them, but they are thrashing about like demons and gnashing their teeth."

"Then the quicker we do it the better," urged Erik. "There is no time for delay. The ships will not be able to hold their position much longer."

Erik's three Norse horses, small but sturdy, were easy to spot among the mass of half-starved animals: they were the only ones that looked well nourished. He had been a little self-indulgent on their last trip and bought the horses for his children. Two of them at least were now surplus stock, although they would certainly have a use if, and when, new land was found. Knud approached the shaggy grey that had been intended for Ulf.

"I take it you will sacrifice Ulf's horse as it's no longer needed," he asked. But Erik shook his head.

"No. Ulf has already paid his price. We will keep his horse in his honour. Gorm is fit and healthy and can make good use of his. We will take Freyja's roan. Only the Gods know if she will ever be fit enough to ride again, and she needs the help of the gods more than any of us."

Mad with fear, its eyes rolling and froth streaming from its mouth, the beast was soothed by Erik's gentle approach and kind words. He felt for his knife, as it stretched its neck towards him.

"Be ready with buckets to catch the blood," he said to his brothers as, quickly and cleanly, he sliced his knife across its throat.

As the blood flowed and the buckets were filled, Erik dipped his hand into the gore and daubed the forehead of the beast.

"I give you thanks for your life and offer you to the great god of the sea, Njord, and Thor, the god of the sky, asking their favour to deliver us from their anger, and to grant peace to the realms of the sea and skies."

Following his lead, Roar and Knud did likewise, before the dying creature was hauled on a pulley to be dropped into the angry sea, the splash barely registering above the roar of the furious waves.

As Erik and Roar prepared to return to their ships, Erik issued one last command.

"We will each make certain that everyone on board our ships will bear the mark of sacrifice for protection. Then the ships will be painted in blood."

The gods accepted the offering. By morning the skies were clear and the storm had passed. The lord of the sky proved even more gracious, for the winds had blown the ships closer to landfall than they had believed possible. Angleland was but a day's sailing away. Furthermore, Freyja had ceased her screaming, though she *was still fretful and her hair was damp from a feverish sweat as she slept. All those on board the three ships rejoiced and gave thanks to the gods Njord and Thor.*

15

Reflections

Freya also awoke to find the sun streaming through her window and no sign of the discomfort she had felt during the night. She was grateful, however, that she had made no plans for the day. The dreams had been so compelling, she needed time to think.

She took a long, rambling walk with Fen and Arty, during which she gave herself time to consider the dreams and attempted to analyse their meaning. The process was far too complicated, raising more questions than she could answer. She tried to shake them off, re-focusing her attention on the wolves as she groomed and fed them after returning to the cottage, but it was no good. The graphic content and flowing narrative of the dreams enthralled her. She needed to understand what they meant, if indeed they meant anything at all.

She spent the rest of the morning drinking endless cups of coffee as she recorded in her dream diary every detail she could recall. She read it through several times, unable to deny there was a definite narrative, filled with personal details of events and family of which she could have no knowledge, not even in her imagination. Nothing like this had come up in her searches for the history of the Sentinel and Sentinel Cottage. Could any of these details be traced to a recorded source?

She made a note of this question on a separate page of the diary. Then she wrote and underlined another:

<u>Who was Erik?</u>

Beneath this she added four headings: Occupation; From; Family; Life Events. Then she trawled once more through her dream record, picking out details for each section, until she cobbled together the basics into a concise format she could easily and quickly assimilate.

Occupation:
    Farmer/trader

Owner of 3 ships

From:

Norway. Village on water's edge
Made up of farmers, crafters, traders

Family:

Wife	Astrid
Children	Bjorn, eldest son
	Ulf, second son
	Gorm, youngest son
	Thurid, elder daughter
	Freyja, youngest child
Roar and Knud	Erik's younger brothers
Ravna	Astrid's grandmother

Life events:

Never-ending winter

Village facing famine

Leads trading expedition to buy supplies to get the village through until the following spring. Bjorn, Roar and Knud accompany him, together with most of the able-bodied men of the village

Village attacked

Astrid is killed

Thurid eldest daughter enslaved

Ulf killed in attack

Gorm survives attack – had led the livestock to the forest

Freyja survives attack in shock; had been hidden beneath her mother's body but had witnessed all

Hardly anyone in the village or among Erik's crew has not suffered a loss

Aftermath: Dead accounted for. Survivors found, sick and injured treated. The missing assumed to have been enslaved. Plans made to sail and search for them

Erik consults the Seidr for healing of Freyja with magic and ceremony

Funeral pyres. Erik misses the ceremony, the price charged by the Seidr

Erik's plans with Bjorn, to sail to seek Thurid, expanded to
include all who wish to join the search for their own
loved ones, and those who wish to leave the village
for safety. Erik's ships made available to all. The
cargo gathered to be equally divided among the
survivors
Erik to take Astrid's and Ulf's ashes with him. Promises her
the remains will be buried beneath a sacred tree
The voyage to England: mostly fair weather, hits a storm
Freyja badly affected by seasickness? Her condition
worsens
Erik makes sacrifice of horse

Apart from mention of interring the ashes of Astrid and Ulf
beneath a tree (which could be one of many ancient trees in England
or elsewhere), there was nothing to link any of the information
directly with the Sentinel. Nevertheless, it was the only clue Freya
had, so she made and underlined another note:

Could the Sentinel be the burial place of Astrid and Ulf? Did Erik
settle in England? Is he real?

Freya let her pen drop and rubbed her hands over her face,
before pressing them into her aching back. She had been working
on the dream diary all day, with very little to eat at breakfast; now
she was surprised to notice it was mid-afternoon. Leaving the diary
on the table, she made herself some sandwiches and a fresh pot of
tea, carrying them outside on to the patio.
As she ate, she breathed in the fresh air and let it clear her
senses. But she could do nothing about the thoughts that skipped and
ran uncontrollably through her mind. Not even taking Fen and Arty
for their exercise after lunch could shift her focus, though the wolves
revelled in the cooling breeze and the scents of the summer pastures.
When she eventually returned to the cottage and had settled
Fen and Arty, she spent some time preparing a one-pot meal for tea.
Leaving it to cook slowly, she began to work once more on the
dream diary, adding to the list of questions.

Aston – Talks a lot about Erik in connection with the Sentinel. (Not shared my dreams with him.) Where did he get the name and idea from?

Was finding the Sentinel a random act? Possibly, but I don't think it was

Was finding the Sentinel meant to be? Possibly, I think, yes. Everything fitted into place to make it possible. The lottery win, the chance (fated) discovery of the Sentinel and Sentinel Cottage conveniently being on the market. The chance (fated) meeting with David and Colonel Winguard's eager agreement to a quick, favourable sale. New people in my life who supporting me in my new life. Too many factors fit into place, can't be random

Was I called home? Meant to be?

Was there a purpose? Yes, the Sentinel needed to be protected from developers.

Connections?

There was one disturbing thought that Freya deliberately omitted from her list. It concerned Màné. The image of the Seidr in her dream bearing Màné's face disturbed her, yet she felt a strong pull towards the young woman. The problem was she still had doubts whether Màné would prove to be a source of help or danger. She could not, in all conscience, commit such thoughts to paper. It could be defamatory. She closed the diary and put it away, wondering whether further dreams would bring her more answers.

Yet it seemed the dreams had stopped. Four nights passed during which Freya slept undisturbed. Then came a day when there was no time to dwell on dreams or their lack.

16

Exciting Times and High Expectations

Today was a big day for all the family. Freya was taking Aston to the children's camp, while Marie was taking Rose to check out student digs. Although Rose had been granted a place at the University of Leeds, she had opted to accept a place at York instead, where she could study Law and Criminology. It was an exciting time for them all and they were travelling to York together. On such a day Freya didn't know why, but as Marie pulled up in the driveway, she shoved her dream diary into her handbag at the last minute.

As they headed towards York, Freya tried to keep up with the chatter of both her grandchildren – Rose full of excitement for the future and Aston full of the excitement of embracing the past. Marie dropped Aston and Freya off at the entrance to the ruins of St Mary's Abbey, which now stood in the grounds of the York Museum. Neither Freya nor Marie knew where the day would lead, so they made no arrangements to meet up for lunch, but before driving off, Marie said, "Message me when you're ready and I'll come pick you both up."

"Good luck, Rose," Freya called after them and waved frantically.

There was no shortage of wannabe Vikings of all ages making their way towards the camp area. Aston kept running ahead, then returning to urge Freya to "Hurry up, Nan! We'll be late."

They were in plenty of time for registration. Rollo and Màné were only two of many tasked with organising the process of directing the children to where they needed to be and dealing with the concerns of parents and guardians. When Aston spotted them, he impolitely ignored the young man who had begun to check his details and ran off, shouting, "Rollo! Màné! I'm here!"

Freya apologised to the abandoned volunteer before catching up with Aston. She was an indulgent grandmother, but she would not tolerate rudeness.

"Aston, just to be clear. Rollo is not here to personally supervise you, and if you are rude and disobedient to others charged with your care, I will take you home. Do you understand?"

For a few seconds Aston looked contrite.

"I'm sorry, Nan," he murmured. But then he caught sight of Rollo's conspiratorial wink and the smile returned to his face.

"I'll show this young warrior where to go and leave you in Màné's capable hands, Ms Fraser. She'll be happy to answer any concerns you may have."

As Aston sped off beside Rollo without a backward glance, Freya found herself under intense scrutiny by Màné. The young woman tucked her arm through Freya's.

"Let's grab a coffee," she said. "I'm free this morning now the registrations are over. I think we have much to talk about." She led Freya away from the registration area to a tent providing refreshments.

"A coffee would be lovely, thank you. But I have no real concerns to raise," Freya assured her.

Màné smiled. "Ah, but I have much to discuss with you, as it happens. Grab a table and I'll fetch the coffees."

Intrigued, Freya did as she was bid.

"We only have instant coffee on offer, I'm afraid," Màné said as she set the cups and a plate of oat cakes on the table. "Now, would you describe yourself as a spiritual or a practical person, Ms Fraser?"

Surprised by the question, Freya hesitated only briefly before responding.

"Please call me Freya. And I would say practical without hesitation. Why?"

"Because I can see you need help and I want to know how best to give it to you." Màné spoke quietly. "I believe you are being haunted. Messages are being directed towards you but are causing you much concern. Am I close to the truth?"

"Can I be honest, Màné? I think haunted is probably the wrong word." Freya took a deep breath, surprising herself by choosing to be frank in her response,

" Like Aston, I've become absorbed in the history of the Sentinel and the land it stands on. Researching it and supporting

103

Aston has become almost an obsession. I have many questions and few answers as it happens, which plays on my mind."

Màné shook her head. "No, it is more than that, I believe. You can be honest with me, Freya. If you are, I can help you or guide you to another who can give practical help. You can trust me."

Freya sighed and resigned herself to sharing the dream diary with Màné. Hadn't this been what she was half hoping for when she shoved the notebook into her bag this morning? Fumbling in its depths, she pulled the diary out and handed it to her companion.

"Dreams. A sort of serial narrative that plays out when I sleep. Each one carries on from the last. I don't know what to make of them."

Holding the diary, Màné looked questioningly at Freya.

"May I?"

"Of course."

Freya passed an anxious half hour as Màné became absorbed in the diary. To pass the time, she worked her way through the plate of oat cakes, only realising she had eaten them all when Màné looked up.

"This is incredible! But dreams are difficult to analyse. On the face of it, I would say Erik is communicating with you. He is sharing his story. But dreams cannot always be taken at face value. You obviously have an idea of where you want to go and what you want to discover from a practical point of view, so let's take that route as our starting point."

"But how? Where would I start?" Freya's voice held a pleading note. "Between us, I think Aston and I have exhausted the online sources and libraries. I have no idea where else to look."

Màné smiled a little sheepishly.

"As it happens, I know the very person who is already eager to help you and Aston with your research. I know Rollo meant to speak to you about it. He shared Aston's assignment with his friend, Citric Olafson, a research fellow at York University. He specialises in the Danelaw area surrounding York. He thinks Aston's work, with a bit more research, could well be worth publishing. If there is anything in the records to verify Erik's existence locally, he'll know about it."

"Oh, my goodness! That's amazing. Are you serious? Aston's work is that good? He's eleven and he catches the attention of a research fellow at the university? Are you truly serious?" Freya covered her hot cheeks with her hands, flushed with pride at Aston's achievement.

Màné smiled again, her silver-grey eyes sparkling.

"I'm deadly serious. I knew it was a good piece of research, well put together. But even I didn't think Citric's opinion of it would be so high. He's going to be here later today, so I'll make sure you and Aston get to meet him. Finding anything out about Erik will be exciting.

"I have a group to lead.so I hope you'll excuse me Freya. You will be around this afternoon when the camp ends, won't you, Freya? I'll look out for you here when Citric arrives."

Once the younger woman had left, Freya telephoned Marie to let her know the amazing news. Marie was as flabbergasted as her mother.

"What? Aston's assignment is getting published?"

"With a little more research, yes, quite possibly."

"Don't agree to anything without me being there. You're far too trusting. Let me know when this professor arrives, and I'll be there in ten or fifteen minutes."

Freya agreed. It was only right that any decisions should involve Marie, and she would make that clear.

The August day was a scorcher. By the time she wandered around The Shambles, weaving in between the crowds along the narrow streets, she decided to give the pub and restaurants a miss. Electing instead to buy a pic-nic lunch to eat in Museum Gardens since she wanted to ensure she didn't miss seeing Citric, or be late for Aston. Finishing her lunch, Freya wandered through the remains of the ancient Saint Mary's Abbey. Somehow, after all the passing centuries and the criminal destruction by Henry VIII, it still retained a sense of peace, a sense of sanctuary. After a while, Freya settled herself on a wooden bench in the shadow of a tree and let the peace wash over her. She needed it.

Freya jerked awake (had she even been asleep?) as the bench she was resting on bounced as someone added their weight to it.

"Wake up, Nan. You look like a tramp!" she heard Rose say.

She gathered her senses.

"No need to be rude, young lady. I wasn't asleep. I was just resting my eyes from the sun. Why are you here already? Are you sorted with student digs?"

Rose smiled and kissed Freya on the cheek by way of apology.

"Yes, all sorted. I've got a great room in the halls, and I've met a few of the other students who'll be there too. I'm getting excited now. It won't be long before I start."

Freya gathered her into a warm embrace.

"That's wonderful. I'm so pleased. How did you grow up so fast?"

Rose ignored the question and continued to tease her grandmother.

"You were asleep! It's almost five o'clock [and the sun has moved. it's shady here now." Rose laughed before going on. "Mum and that professor guy are waiting for you. Come on!"

Only slightly abashed, Freya linked arms with her granddaughter and together they made their way back to the camp. They found Marie and Professor Olafson in the refreshment tent, talking animatedly. As Freya and Rose approached, Marie stood up.

"The wanderer returns! Professor, this is my mother, Freya Fraser."

Professor Olafson rose quickly and met Freya with an eagerly outstretched hand.

"I'm very pleased to meet you, Ms Fraser. Your nurturing of Aston's interest in Norse history is most admirable."

Freya responded with a smile.

"It's actually the other way around, Professor. Aston has done most of the research himself and kindly shared it with me. I've done very little. Though it has become a shared interest. I find it fascinates me as much as it does Aston."

The professor pulled a seat out for Freya to join them at the table. Rose obligingly went to order fresh coffees all round, before taking herself off to collect Aston from the activity area, so the adults could continue their discussion.

The professor picked up the conversation.

"Aston has done a remarkable job of collecting and co-ordinating the known and mythological facts of an otherwise untouched area of study. I understand his interest was sparked by your recent purchase of land associated with a Norse settlement, a settlement that, until now, has attracted no form of professional study. Is that correct?"

"None to my knowledge," Freya replied.

Before the professor could add anything else to the conversation, Aston burst upon them, full of unbridled excitement about his day.

"I'm starving," he declared. "I could eat a plateful of Hogsnott. What's for tea?"

Marie was not impressed by his rude entrance.

"Calm down and mind your manners, Aston. This is Professor Olafson. He's an expert on Norse history here in Yorkshire and he would like to talk to you about your assignment. Sit down nicely."

The professor shook Aston by the hand.

"Congratulations on an outstanding piece of work, young man. I have a proposition to make to you, but far be it for me to stand in the way of a warrior's hunger." He directed his next words to Freya and Marie. "I'm not sure when I'll be free next, but I would like to make some progress today. Would it be a great imposition if I invited you all to join me for an early supper to continue exploring the best way to take Aston's work forward?"

Naturally, they all agreed.

For the most part, Freya, Marie and Rose were little more than onlookers, as the professor engaged Aston in conversation. Eventually, Rose excused herself, pleading an arrangement to meet up with some of her new housemates, while Marie wished the professor would get on with it, whatever "it" was going to be. So far, he had shown a great deal of uncommitted interest, but had offered no direct advice to help Aston move forward, and there had been no suggestion that the assignment was worth publishing. But then, as the waitress cleared away their dessert plates, the professor took a notebook out of his jacket pocket.

"So, now we have the civilities out of the way, let's get down to business, shall we, Aston?" he said, with a smile that embraced Freya and Marie as well as Aston. "In the eyes of your mother, grandmother, and the law, you are a child, and society places little expectation on the accomplishments or abilities of children. Yet their accomplishments are valued nevertheless."

Aston looked a little uncertain. Freya bridled.

"I can assure you, Professor, we are very proud of what Aston has accomplished and the dedication and effort he has put into his assignment." She felt it was her duty to make her point very clear.

The professor, undaunted, went on.

"I have no doubt of it, Freya," they had started to use first names early in the evening, "and rightly so. It is a commendable piece of work. For that reason, I have no intention of treating Aston as a child. In my opinion, he will benefit most by learning, using and developing the same principles of research that I expect of my students."

"He's only eleven years old," Marie reminded the professor, who remained as determined and as undaunted as ever.

"I haven't forgotten that, Marie, but thank you for reinforcing my opinion that what we expect from children is limited by their chronological age. It shouldn't be." He returned his attention directly to Aston.

"You are a bright and intelligent young man, Aston, and a very fortunate one, in my opinion. Your grandmother will nurture you, your mother will defend you and I will mentor you, if that is what you want. Is it?"

Aston looked around the table. Freya gave him an almost imperceptible nod, Marie smiled, and the professor watched him closely. Aston made his mind up.

"I think I'd like that. What do you want me to do, Professor?"

"Well, Aston, the first thing I teach my students is that good research relies on using credible sources, ones that can be referenced and verified. The internet is a useful tool, but not always reliable in the accuracy of its information. So, firstly, I would advise you to go over your sources and check on their reliability. You will, of course, need some guidance, so I propose to give you full access to my own database with one of my students to aid you in its use. If that is acceptable to you and your mother and grandmother, naturally. I will make my office available to you from next week. So, what do you think? Have you any questions?"

"Can Nan come with me?"

"Of course, if she and your mother are agreeable."

Freya and Marie agreed readily, and the arrangements were finalised. As they were taking their leave of the professor, he had one more piece of advice for Aston.

"No matter what others expect of you, Aston, always have the highest expectations of yourself."

17

Viking Summer

Aston, with Freya's support, spent the rest of the summer immersed in Norse history. The week after he completed the children's camp, he had committed himself to being a full member of the re-enactors group run by Rollo and Màné. Then he took up the professor's offer. The professor had proved as good as his word, setting aside two afternoons a week (Wednesdays and Fridays) when Aston could have the use of his office and database, under the supervision and guidance of a young postgrad student named Connor MacPherson. Freya and Aston liked the young Scot on sight as he welcomed them on their first visit with a smile that could have lit up the world.

"Aston! My wee partner. Welcome! And don't look so pensive. We're going to be equals in this enterprise – a fifty–fifty partnership, sharing our knowledge and skills to produce something special. Agreed?"

Aston looked doubtful, giving a shrug, though he returned Connor's smile.

"You'll know a lot more than me. I just know about the Sentinel and Erik."

"I know how to access information from the professor's database, which is what I'm here to teach you. You certainly know more about the Sentinel and the settlement you've discovered than I do, and that's what you'll teach me. I'll be guided by you as far as that's concerned. So, are we agreed, partner?" To seal the deal, Connor held out his hand, which Aston shook. Connor turned his attention to Freya.

"Thank you for delivering Aston safely, Ms Fraser. Your work for the moment is done. Not that I'm dismissing you in any way. You're most welcome to stay and observe. There's a wee kitchenette just through that door to your left. Feel free to help yourself to drinks and snacks."

Freya was not unaware that she had just been put firmly, if gently, in her place. She had no part in this partnership and was not to interfere with the process. Having established the pecking order, Connor settled Aston and himself at the professor's desk.

"Professor Olafson has left us some guidelines on what he wants us to get through this week. So, let's go through them together first, then you can take me through your assignment, and we can start to get things done."

In no time the two of them had their heads bent over their work, with one or the other busily making notes. Freya quietly retired for a coffee in the kitchenette.

Following that initial session, Freya decided to simply drop Aston off for future afternoons with Connor. There was no point in wasting her time lurking in the kitchenette when she could use it to better advantage exploring the Norse remnants of York's past. While escorting Aston to the re-enactors children's camp, she had discovered that the area that was now Museum Gardens had formerly been the main site of Norse administration for the Danelaw. Located outside the city walls, it had been the home of the Jarls, the ruling nobility, and subsequently named Jarlstown or Earlstown. As a point of reference, Freya made it her first port of call. Of course, there was nothing to see other than the peaceful beauty of twenty-first-century parkland. All visual traces of Jarlstown and its inhabitants had been erased.

Freya would never have thought of herself as either a spiritual or fanciful person, but she could not deny the connection she felt with the Sentinel, nor where responding to that connection had led her. It was neither fanciful nor imagined – it was real. Another thing she realised since her visit to the Jorvik Viking Centre was that what is visible on the surface to the naked eye is not the only reality. Beneath the modern street of Coppergate, the lives of the people who had lived in the area during the tenth century had waited patiently to be revealed. So, she walked along the pathways of Museum Gardens and let her mind drift to the Jarls who ruled from there in the name of their king. What responsibilities would they have had? Keeping law and order almost certainly; settling land disputes and collecting taxes would be a high priority, perhaps licensing or monitoring markets and traders? Such things would normally generate paperwork, lists, deeds of ownership, but the Norse were not known for leaving written records, and of the records they had left, few had survived. She hoped Aston would turn up something in the professor's database. Maybe she should also chase up the librarian at Northallerton who had promised to look for more evidence on the Sentinel. Yes, she determined. That's exactly what she should do.

Looking up from her reverie, Freya found herself standing on the path to the ancient church of St Olave, another link with the Viking past, with the patron saint of Norway still standing guard over the arched window above the doorway. She tried the door only to find it locked.

"What is it that you seek?"

Freya swivelled around at the sound of the unexpected voice. She found herself face to face with a tall, slim man, dressed entirely in black. His long hair (was it grey or palest blonde?) was tied back in a ponytail, looped at the top to form a topknot. Guessing his age at between forty and fifty, Freya assumed him to be the priest. She smiled.

"What I am seeking is the answer to so many questions I haven't even formed yet. Sorry for the wishy-washy answer, but everything in my life is a bit wishy-washy at the moment. All smoke and mirrors."

He returned her smile, though his own held a hint of sadness – or maybe it was sympathy.

"Walk with me. I will tell you the history of the church, while you gather your thoughts." He began by pointing at St Olave's statue.

"St Olave was not born to be a saint. For most of his life he wasn't even a Christian, but a pagan Viking warrior. A very accomplished warrior, as it happens."

"Really? In what way was he accomplished?" Freya asked.

The man gave a sheepish grin, before replying, "I suppose, depending on your perspective, he could also be described as notorious. He led a warband of ships up the river Thames and destroyed London Bridge, while supporting the claim of Æthelred the Unready against Cnut. Eventually, when Cnut gained the upper hand, Olave took himself back to Norway, where he harried the Norse into becoming Christians, earning for himself a sainthood and the recognition of being the country's patron saint."

They had been walking round the perimeter of the church as they talked, Freya glanced up at the grey stone edifice of the tower, crowned with finials which, to her mind, resembled the iconic misconception of the horns on a Viking helmet.

"Presumably he founded this church before he left," she said.

"I'm afraid not. The cult of St Olave caught on quickly among the Norsemen. The original church on this site named for St Olave was founded by Siward, Earl of Northumbria, who ruled the Danelaw in this area. It has been altered over time. This building mostly dates from the fifteenth century. Siward is buried within the church, according to tradition."

"Is he really? Wow! I'd love to see inside." She hoped he would volunteer, as the vicar, to open the church for her, but no offer was extended. Taking the hint, she glanced at her watch and made her excuses. "Gosh! It's much later than I thought. I have my grandson to collect. But thank you so much for your time. I've learned a lot from our conversation."

She extended her hand, which he took.

"The pleasure was mine."

She was walking away when he called after her, "Freya Freyjasdottir!"

She turned without registering the misnomer. Then her smile slid from her face. He was but a few feet away, and only seconds had passed, but something about him had changed. It was as though his face had been overlaid by another, similar, but younger face. She gasped in shock, covering her mouth with her hand. She recognised him from her dreams. It was Knud, Erik's brother. She could not find words, but he did.

"Listen to my brother and your unspoken questions will be answered."

He turned, walking quickly away until he was suddenly gone from sight.

The pounding of her heart eased as she made her way back to the university, as her rational mind rejigged the memory so she could make sense of it. It had been nothing but a trick of her imagination, surely. By the time she collected Aston, she had pushed the encounter to the back of her mind.

As they travelled home, Aston was eager to update Freya on his progress.

"I've finished editing the sources now. A lot of the ones I

113

found online are a bit vague and have no foundation on traceable evidence, so I've edited them out. Connor says it's important to use only sources that can be verified or checked."

He spoke like a seasoned academic, causing Freya to hide her smile.

"That sounds like a good idea. So, what's the next step? What are your plans for next week?"

"I need to tighten up the historical background, edit out a lot of the general history which falls out of the focus timeline. "

"That sounds like a big job. I didn't know you had a focused timeline. What is it going to be?"

Aston gave a shrug.

"It won't be that hard, Nan. I'll just cut the bits I don't need straight away and paste them into a blank document for storage. Connor thinks the best starting point will be the dated document showing the Sentinel on Heimdall's land. That's dated 946, so ten years before and after would be a good, focused period to search for other documents related to the settlement. And to build up an accurate historical timeline at the same time."

Freya was genuinely impressed and reached across to grasp his hand,

"It sounds like you have this nailed. I'm very proud of you, Aston. Very proud indeed."

As Freya pulled up outside Marie's house, Marie hurried down the path to greet them.

"I hope you're not planning on a quick escape. I've got an extra-large lasagne to get through." She smiled at her mother, opening the driver's door to allow no chance for refusal.

"I was planning on getting home to the boys, but that offer is far too tempting to refuse. Thank you." Freya accepted gracefully, as she climbed out of the car. Aston was already out and heading up the stairs to his room.

Marie tucked her arm beneath her mother's as they walked up the path to the house.

"So, how did it go with Connor today? Were you still 'surplus to requirements?'"

"Even us old girls have our pride! I never gave them the chance to side-line me today. I dopped Aston off and left them to it, while I treated myself to some 'me' time, wandering around in the sunshine." Freya laughed.

"Really? Didn't Aston mind?"

"Not in the least. He didn't even look up when I left. After all the upset with Miss Carey, I think this is exactly what he needs. He's got all his enthusiasm back, and wait till he tells you his plans. You'll be amazed."

The smell of the freshly cooked lasagne must have drifted up the stairs, as Aston came clattering down just in time to help lay the table. He was still eager to chat about his project.

"I've sent you the new file with the changes on, Nan. Will you read it and check it's OK when you get home? Connor's great, but you know more about our project than he does."

Freya felt redeemed. She wasn't surplus to requirements after all.

18

More from Erik

Erik returned to Freya that night. She recognised the dreamscape immediately. His ships were drawing close to the shoreline of Whitby, travelling slowly west towards Sandsend and Lythe.

High on the clifftop the original abbey of Whitby was a burnt-out ruin, abandoned, yet keeping a glowering watch out to sea. Townspeople had gathered on the stony beach. Some had witnessed the ships' struggles against the storm and had come to offer help. Others had arrived to defend their towns and villages from would-be raiders. Viking ships invariably brought fear in their wake, although many came to trade at the market at Sandsend. The ships weighed anchor off the shoreline, and only Erik made his way to the beach, wading ashore, his arms held high.

"Good people, we mean you no harm. My name is Erik the Trader. My ships carry women and children, seeking a place of safety. I would speak to your Jarl or village elders."

A man, better dressed than most of those present, stepped forward.

"I am Osric, elected speaker of this area and master of the ports. I represent the king's authority. I will speak with you if you will come with me."

Erik followed Osric up a steep path to a longhouse in the village, with most of those present on the beach following them and taking seats around the edges. Osric sat on a seat in the centre of the room, but Erik was left standing.

"So, Erik the Trader, why are you really here? What is it you want?"

Erik spread his hands, a sign of honesty.

"It is as I told you. My ships carry families – women, children and aged folk, who seek a new life and a place of safety."

"Why do they need this from us? What is wrong with your own lands? Why have they been driven out? Perhaps you bring death and sickness in your ships."

"Lord, you have many questions that deserve an honest answer, which I will give you in full. But let me begin by assuring you, and all these honest men here, that my ships hold no danger to your community. My story will not be short, so perhaps you would be kind enough to give me a drink before I start, so my words do not dry up my throat."

Osric nodded and a thrall hurried forward to press a horn of watered mead into Erik's hands. Erik took several thirsty gulps from it before commencing his harrowing story.

There was total silence as Erik spoke, which broke into whispered muttering as he described the hardship of the never-ending winter which stole away spring, followed by the summer of unceasing rain.

"The ground was too hard and frozen to sow a harvest. When at last the thaw came, rain came also and washed away the seeds we managed to get into the ground. There would be no harvest and we faced a new winter of starvation." Erik paused to take another drink, as several men stood to voice their opinions.

"He speaks the truth," one mad said. "We have heard many reports from traders of this never-ending winter."

Other voices were less sympathetic.

"Aye, we have heard the stories. And now we know the truth of why he has brought his ships here – to plunder our own winter stores, leaving us to starve while he grows fat on our labour. I denounce him as a trickster led by Loki."

Rumbles of dissent increased before Osric restored the room to silence. Then he addressed Erik.

"You stand accused of deceit and trickery, Erik the Trader. You may respond."

"My response lies in the completion of my story, which, with your permission, Lord, I will continue." He waited for Osric's nod of consent before restarting.

"I now know there are worse deaths than starvation, but as we gathered in the Thingstead to decide our fate, it was the prospect of starvation that focused the mind of every man present. The question was, how could we protect our families from such a fate?"

As he continued, Erik walked around the room, looking each man in the eye as he spoke.

117

"You are wise to be cautious. Would that I had given more thought to the safety of my family and my village when I should have done. But I did not. One voice was raised in favour of raiding tactics to secure supplies against the coming winter. It was quickly dismissed. I volunteered to take my ships on a trading mission. Everyone contributed what they could for a fair trade, and every able-bodied man accompanied me to man the ships. It was a good plan, a successful plan. But we left behind the women and children, the frail, old and sick, with no protection except the wisdom of the Gothi. That was our mistake."

Turning away from the general gathering, Erik addressed Osric once more, as he described the brutality of the raid they had discovered when they returned home.

"Every man on my ships suffered a loss. Not one family survived untouched. We honoured our dead and gathered together the living. Some will recover, some will not, but it is these survivors I carry on my ships. We have heard the kingdom of Jorvik is a haven for the Norse, Lord Osric. If it is in your power to offer protection and safety to those who would settle here, I implore you to be merciful."

For the space of a minute, which seemed endless to Erik, Osric held his gaze. Finally, his decision made, he stood.

"I make you no promises, Erik the Trader. I will visit your ships and assess the situation for myself. Then we will talk again. In the meantime, I must ask you to return to your ships and ensure your people stay there for now. If you need anything for the immediate comfort of the women and children – food, fresh water or medication – I will have it sent across."

Before sweeping out, Osric appointed a small escort to see Erik back to his ship, bidding them to make a note of any immediate needs. Erik requested that the animals be removed from his ships for grazing on the common land under Osric's protection, with two of Erik's men to watch over them.

The scene changed

Osric presided over his feasting table. The feast in question was intended to honour Erik and his brothers, while at the same time *gathering further information. Erik knew how this worked. He also knew his manners. He stood to make a short speech to his host.*

"Lord Osric, I extend the thanks of all those on my ships who have benefited from your kindness and generosity in providing immediate comforts for the women and children especially, but also the same for the animals we carried with us. They are sorry-looking beasts, but now they can have proper grazing, they will thrive, I am sure. Those who wish to settle will need to work hard to make a new life for themselves, but healthy beasts will help to give them a good start."

If Erik intended to say more, he was cut short by Knud, who raised his drinking horn to Osric.

"My especial thanks to you, Lord, for allowing me to walk the deck of my ship without standing in animal droppings. Skol!"

The hall erupted into laughter. Osric joined in. But he did not want the traders to think he would meet all their requests without question. This was a serious business and he still had concerns.

"It is my pleasure and my duty to help where I can. But my greatest duty is to preserve the safety of my own territory. Along with the settlers, you have three fully crewed ships, and this is something I cannot overlook, for it amounts to what could become a small army set loose on my territory."

Clearly this had not occurred to any of the brothers. They all spoke at once in an attempt to reassure Osric that his fears were unfounded.

"The crews will remain with the ships and will be leaving once we have found a refuge for the settlers," Erik began.

"It is not just the settlers we are concerned with. Many of our families and neighbours were enslaved by the raiders. We have vowed to rescue them. All the ships and the crews will be leaving." Knud sounded surprised that this wasn't already known.

Roar directed his words directly to Erik. "Why did you not make it clear that the ships would be leaving? Have you not asked about the red-sailed ships that we seek?"

Erik held his hands up placatingly to his brothers.

"Be at peace, both of you. If I have been remiss, I apologise to you both, as I do to you also, Lord Osric. I have been considering the matter as a separate issue to the settlers. But if I had spoken

earlier, I could have spared your concerns, Lord. I beg your pardon."

Osric merely nodded an acknowledgement, as a voice from somewhere down the table spoke out.

"The red-sailed ships you speak of passed by two days before you arrived. We gathered on the beach with Lord Osric and would not let them land. They sailed on, likely headed for Irland."

"That puts them five days ahead of us. If we are to have any chance of catching them, we cannot delay further. Lord Osric, is there no way you can accommodate the settlers? You have seen them for yourself. They can bring no trouble to your lands." Roar appealed directly to their host.

"I will hold a meeting of the Thing tomorrow. You will have your answer then. Now let us feast as friends and be merry."

Freya sat up, turned over and let sleep reclaim her.

Many small fishing coracles were making their way to and from Erik's ships, ferrying the settlers ashore. Those who had already landed gathered close together on the pebbled beach, unsure as to what to expect now they were on foreign soil. Erik, with Freyja in his arms, was the last to leave the ship after bidding Bjorn, Roar and Knud farewell. It had not been easy for any of them. Bjorn especially was not ready to lose the guidance of his father. As Erik turned away, Bjorn called after him.

"You swore to my mother that you would continue to guide me. Am I less your child than Gorm and Freyja?"

Erik hesitated, torn between the pleas of his eldest son and the immediate needs of his youngest children.

"You are almost a man, but you will always be my son. I have provided all you need to thrive. The ships are yours. Your uncles will continue to guide you. You are not alone, my child. For you to take up my task and seek out your sister will make me proud. I know I am represented by such a fine son. I also promised your mother that I would care for Gorm, Freyja and Grandmother Ravna. They cannot travel further, and they have no one else to provide for them. My task now is to find them a safe home and care for them, just as I have cared for you. You can come with me, but

you will be walking away from your destiny. Think hard now before you decide."

Bjorn made a move towards his father, but Roar shot out his hand and held him back.

"Nephew, it is time to put childhood behind you and embrace the gift of manhood. This is where you are needed. This is your fate, and you cannot reject it."

As Bjorn hesitated, Erik turned away, lowering himself and Freyja into the last awaiting coracle. He did not look back as it was rowed to the shore, though his heart was heavy as he left Bjorn behind. He had thought to share his son's journey along the way to manhood – to always be there to advise and guide him – but it could not be.

19

Securing the Future

Freya emerged slowly from sleep, wanting to continue her dream and follow Erik, but now, both sleep and the dream eluded her. Another day had dawned, and she had things to do, before meeting David for lunch.

The Sign of the Two Wolves was packed. It was fortunate that David had pre-booked their table. Ever the gentleman, he rose as soon as she entered, giving her a warm but chaste kiss on the cheek, then holding her chair out as she sat.

"It's wonderful to see you, Freya. It seems so long since we last caught up. Are you well?"

"I'm very well, thank you, David. And I agree, a catch-up is way overdue."

Impatient as ever, she was longing to ask him if he had news of the land she was interested in. However, the waiter arrived to take their order, quickly followed by the wine waiter, forcing her to hold her questions in check while he reeled off an impressive list of wine and other alcoholic beverages, David and Freya both stuck with sparkling water since they were driving, and the wine waiter was not impressed. Throughout the meal, David kept the conversation on neutral ground, impressed with what Freya told him about Aston's new lines of enquiry. Eventually, she was forced to ask her question.

"I'm so sorry, David, but I can't bear the suspense any longer. Have you got any news about the land purchases?"

David laughed.

"My lovely Freya! Forgive me for teasing you, but all good things come to those who wait. I have some very positive news, and some not so encouraging." He took a folded piece of paper from his jacket pocket and handed it to her. It showed a rough sketch of her land, with several * symbols on the fields adjacent to the Sentinel. There were four in all: one immediately to the right of the great tree and three to the left.

Freya looked up.

"I'm hoping the stars indicate a willingness to negotiate price?"

"They do, subject to your agreement. I think the price of £7,500 per acre is fair, but the vendor also wants to retain exclusive use of the land for pasturing his sheep. Twenty acres in all, all immediately adjacent to the Sentinel, so the total cost would be £150,000."

Freya didn't hesitate.

"I agree. Having the sheep grazing the land would also be to my benefit."

"Not so fast. My advice would be to agree to exclusive grazing rights, but on a leasehold basis. As a gesture of goodwill, you could offer free grazing for a year, then the lease would be renewable annually at a cost of £2,100 in total, plus the cost of repairs. Any damage to the boundary walls and hedges caused by animals and farm equipment should be paid for by the farmer. Failure to comply would make the lease void. At no point will there be access to the Sentinel's field."

"Oh, I'm so glad I've got your business acumen to lean on. Yes, that sounds like a good plan. Let's do it. How soon can we get the ball rolling?"

"No time like the present." David smiled, pulling his phone out of his pocket.

Surprisingly, his negotiations were not as straightforward as Freya imagined.

"Afternoon, Jack. It's David. I'm with my client. Subject to an inspection of the land, she thinks there is a deal to be done that will suit you both. How about if we come over in about an hour? Perfect, thank you. We'll see you shortly."

"OK, I'm curious," said Freya as he hung up. "Why did you not simply explain the terms? I don't really need to inspect the land."

"Never buy anything unseen, Freya! Besides, if these Yorkshire farmers don't see any hard negotiations, they think they are being done. You are going to be his landlord, so he needs to know you are no pushover. Do you fancy another coffee before we go?"

"Yes, please. I'll just see if Aston is free to join us. He'll be so excited."

An hour later, with Aston in tow, Freya and David, with Jack Jacobson the farmer, were walking the "Top Field", to the immediate right of the Sentinel. It was the biggest acreage of the package and gave a closer, more detailed view of the Sentinel than was visible from the road. For a short time, all four stood and gazed in awe at the ancient oak. Freya, tears suddenly spilling unbidden, choked out, "If that isn't worth saving, then I don't know what is."

"Aye, can't deny it has a presence," said Jack. "But I've no time to stand wasting looking at a tree. Let's get on with this field walk."

Aston was fascinated and couldn't be dragged away, as Freya and David accompanied the farmer around the large perimeter. There was nothing out of place. Calling to Aston, they made their way through the gate to follow a steep, winding footpath that led to the field known as Hill Dip. This emerged to the left of the Sentinel and gave yet another view of it. An idea struck Freya and she decided to sound Jack out on it.

"I've liked all I've seen so far. I'm thinking that, to protect your sheep, I could fence off a small pathway to give private access around the Sentinel. Would you be prepared to allow access to your pathway between the Top Field and this one, Hill Dip, to form a circular viewing route?"

Jack was wary.

"When you say a circular pathway around the tree, you're not planning some sort of pagan ceremonies, like at Stonehenge, are you?

"Oh, good grief, no! Nothing like that at all. My thoughts are for personal, private access only. With the circular access it would be so much easier to monitor the Sentinel for things like storm damage."

Jack was still hesitant, so David stepped in.

"Don't start getting uppity, Jack. Freya would be doing you a favour by fencing off an access route to save disturbing your flock. As the owner she could, of course, have free access whenever she chooses."

"I know the access rights well enough, David, thank you. But I appreciate the consideration. I'll think on it."

Freya had to be content with that for now. There were two more parcels of land to walk: Home View, a small paddock overlooking the valley that sheltered Jack's farm, and, in front of that, Chapel Field, a larger strip of pasture bordering the road. Freya found all to her satisfaction and had to admit Jack kept his land in good order. He would make a good tenant.

David took charge of the formalities, and the two men shook hands.

"Well, thanks for your time, Jack. I'll get Freya's instructions and we'll be in touch shortly."

Freya also took her leave of Jack with a warm handshake.

"I'm really eager to make this work for both of us. Thank you so much for your time."

Then she turned to call to Aston. For an instant she could have sworn he was deep in conversation with a figure standing just over the fence from him, but as he turned in response to her voice and ran towards her, there was only Aston to be seen.

Back in the cottage, David sat copying up his notes to make the formal offer and Aston pored over the diagram the estate agent had made of the land. Freya joined them at the table, bringing drinks – lemonade for Aston and coffee for her and David. As she sat down, Aston waved the sketch at her.

"Can I scan this into my file? The field names may help us discover more information, plus I think it's cool that we've restored at least half of Heimdall's land. You need to buy more on the other side of the river now, Nan."

"We haven't actually bought the land yet," Freya said. "We've just registered our interest. David will make a formal offer when he has everything in place."

Aston turned his attention to David.

"Have you got everything in place now? Ring Mr Jacobson and make the offer, please, David."

David shuffled his paperwork together, looking from Freya to her grandson.

"Everything's noted. I was going to get it all typed up at the office tomorrow before making the formal offer. Let him sweat a bit overnight." Looking at their expectant faces, though, he knew that wasn't going to happen. With a sigh, he pulled out his phone, and Freya and Aston clung to each other in nervous anticipation. Half an hour later, the deal was done, subject to contract. Now it would be up to the solicitors to move things along to completion.

20

Connor MacPherson

As August progressed towards September, Aston put all his efforts into finalising his assignment. He desperately wanted to find some documented evidence that would link the Sentinel and the settlement to the people who had occupied the site all those centuries ago. Together with Connor, he trawled through the professor's database, while Freya chased up her contact at Northallerton library and David gave what time he could to searching the land registry. Between them they were able to piece together a historic record that took them back as far as the early fifteenth century. Fascinating as this was, however, it did not help Aston.

When Freya dropped him off for his penultimate session with Connor during the last week of the summer holidays, they were both surprised to find the professor sitting behind his desk, with no sign of Connor. He looked up as Aston burst through the door without ceremony.

"Ah! Please come in and take a seat, Aston. And I'd be obliged if you would also join us, Freya, if you can spare the time."

"Of course," Freya replied as she took the proffered seat. "It's nice to see you again, Professor."

The professor turned his attention to Aston.

"I've been reviewing your work, Aston. It is an excellent school assignment, but that is all it is, a school assignment…"

If he intended to say more, he was stopped in his tracks by Freya, instantly defensive on Aston's behalf. She almost leapt from her seat and leaned somewhat threateningly on the professor's desk.

"I don't believe Aston's work has been touted as anything but a school assignment, Professor, but that is not 'all it is', and I find such a dismissive remark extremely patronising. For the last three months, he has put his heart and soul into this work. He has conscientiously researched, written and edited his work with dedication equal to any professional academic, but he is only eleven years old. His work is important to him and his family, so no, a school project is not 'all it is'." Freya just about managed to control her anger.

The professor was clearly not used to being challenged. He stared at Freya, clenching and unclenching his hands, but then he relaxed and smiled.

"Freya, I did not intend my words to cause offence and perhaps they were ill chosen. Please forgive me and be seated. My apologies to you also, Aston. If I can continue with what I was going to say, my intention may become clearer."

As Freya resumed her seat, she noticed how shaken and ashen Aston looked. She hoped her outburst hadn't contributed to his discomfort. The professor handed Aston a large brown envelope.

"Connor has told me of your earnest and diligent dedication, Aston. It shows in your work, and it was what led me to offer my help as your mentor. Connor has searched out some documents that may prove useful. If they can be incorporated into your work, it will certainly take it to the next level, and we can discuss a possible publication strategy on your next appointment."

Letting the envelope lie unopened on his knee, Aston asked, "Where is Connor? Why isn't he here?"

The professor looked uncomfortable and hesitated, darting a glance at Freya before he replied. Instinctively, sensing bad news, Freya reached across to hold Aston's hand as the professor replied.

"I'm afraid Connor was in a car accident last night. Thankfully I'm informed he will recover and is comfortable. But he is being cared for in York Hospital."

Aston was distraught. Freya felt his grip tightening in her hand. She now felt appalled at her earlier outburst. This situation could not have been easy for the professor either and she had made it worse.

"Will you take me to see him, Nan?" pleaded Aston. "All his family are in Scotland. and Connor told me they have a farm and it's never easy for them to get away from all the jobs they have to do"

"They may not let us see him today, but we'll go and check how he is and see if he needs anything." Freya gave Aston's hand a reassuring squeeze. Then she apologised to the professor. He was gracious in his response.

"He is the cub of your cub, the child of your child. You have a natural instinct to defend him. Think no more of it."

Taking their leave of the professor, Freya drove the short distance to the hospital. At the reception, they were given directions to Connor's ward. There they were intercepted by a burly male nurse as they approached the nurse's station.

"Visiting hours aren't until three o'clock. Who are you looking for?"

"Connor Macpherson," Freya replied. "He was admitted last night."

The nurse checked on the computer, scrolling down a list of names.

"Are you family?" he asked.

"All his family are farmers in Scotland, it won't be easy for them to get away. We are all he's got." Aston gave the information and Freya added,

"Connor has been like an older brother to my grandson, we want to do all we can for him."

The nurse checked the computer again.

"Well, he's just back from theatre. No visitors today, but you can ring later if you want. Regular visiting hours are 3 to 4 p.m. and 7 to 8."

"He's needed to have surgery?" Aston asked, unable to hide the panic he was feeling. "He is going to be OK, isn't he?"

"He has multiple fractures, so it will take time. But he should be right as rain again in a few months. Don't worry." The nurse smiled reassuringly at Aston.

"I'm guessing he'll need a few things," said Freya. "Will it be all right if we drop them off later today?"

"You can drop them off this afternoon at visiting time." The nurse rummaged through some paperwork and handed her a sheet of paper. "Here's a general list of items for personal care that you may find useful."

There was nothing more to be done but to thank the nurse and depart. Outside the hospital, Freya took a deep breath.

"Well! Today hasn't gone according to plan, has it? Let's go and get something to eat. It'll give us time to gather our thoughts and take a breather."

Much later, their duty to Connor done, they drove home, both saying very little during the journey. Freya was not only shaken by Connor's accident but also embarrassed by her outburst at the professor and uncomfortable that she had lost control in front of Aston.

Aston had his own concerns. He had been shocked and upset by the news of Connor's accident, as they had built up a mutual bond over the past few weeks. But he was also puzzled by the printouts given to him by the professor. Connor and he had scheduled the search for documents and contemporary evidence of the settlement for today, so why had Connor already printed them out? He could not have foreseen his accident. And how had the professor got hold of them? Something didn't sit right with Aston, although he was not ready to put his fears into words.

As they drew up outside Marie's, Freya took her leave, declining Marie's invitation to tea, but promising to let Aston know when they could go to visit Connor. She felt a desperate need for the tranquillity of the homestead and the calm routine of caring for Fen and Arty.

Erik continued to reveal his story that night.

21

The Settlers

They stood on the beach, a raggle-taggle collection of displaced women and children with only a handful of men among them. They watched as the ships sailed away, taking with them their last connection to their homeland.

Erik did not watch the ships leave. He stood with Freyja in his arms, Gorm and Ravna by his side, watching as the townspeople set up their market stalls further along the beach. In the opposite direction, the ruin of Hwitebi Abbey looked out towards the sea, a testament that this land had also suffered from raiders in the past. Would this mean that the people would treat the settlers with compassion or suspicion? There had been mixed sentiments expressed during his interview with Osric, yet Osric had agreed to allow the settlers to land. Erik prayed to the All Father that it was truly an act of goodwill and not a trap.

While the younger children clung to the skirts of their mothers, some of the older ones, free at last from the confines of the ships, used up some of their pent-up energy in running races along the beach, as their mothers shouted, "Stay close! Don't go too far." They came back at speed when three horsemen were seen approaching, with a train of wagons following them. The settlers gathered closer as the leading rider reined in before them.

"My name is Wulfstan," the man announced. "Lord Osric bids you all welcome. Food and shelter wait for you in the Thingstead. The way is steep, so he has provided wagons to transport your goods and chattels, and for the children, aged and sick. Load them up and we will be on our way before the tide comes in."

The Thingstead was warm after the wind-blown beach. Village women had prepared food and welcomed the settlers warmly. Erik found a space beside the fire for Ravna and settled Freyja beside her, then led Gorm to help unload what was theirs from the carts. They didn't have much. Erik had brought only the casks containing the ashes of Astrid and Ulf and three barrels from their share of the winter supplies amassed on his voyage, plus four small bundles of their clothes and personal items. He had burned down their house and everything in it before they left their village. Gorm and he soon had their remaining possessions stashed at the back of the Thingstead.

"What happens now, Father?" Gorm asked. The question revealed the uncertainty he felt about the future, but also his childish confidence that his father would have the answers.

Erik ruffled Gorm's hair.

"Now we wait to see what Lord Osric has planned."

They didn't have long to wait, though Osric didn't arrive alone, and it was clear that in this instance he wasn't the voice of authority. The rich clothes and jewelled brooch of the man who came with him denoted a man of far higher rank than the port keeper. Hovering behind them were two priests, one carrying a small portable table, the other a small box and a roll of vellum. The richly dressed newcomer was not tall, but his stocky build made him appear shorter than he was. His hair was cropped and his face half hidden behind a beard and moustache. When he stepped forward to speak, his voice was not without kindness.

"I am Jarl Svend. My condolences to you, good people, for I know you have suffered much, which is why you find yourselves as strangers in a foreign land seeking a new life, a new beginning. You found a good friend in Osric. He has appealed to me to act on behalf of King Olaf to show you kindness and mercy. I will do that and gladly, though it may not be in the form you envisaged."

He paused as a thrall pressed a drinking horn into his hand and another into Osric's. Jarl Svend took a sip before going on, turning his attention directly to Erik.

"Erik the Trader, I am told you act on behalf of your people. So I ask you, would you become a thrall in order to gain a place of safety for your family?"

Erik stood, glancing around at the people around him.

"You wish to enslave us?"

Jarl Svend held his hands up placatingly.

"If that was my intent, I would have done it already and this discussion would not be taking place. It is a rhetorical question only. What would your answer be?"

Erik signalled for Gorm and Ravna, with Freyja in her arms, to stand beside him before he answered.

"I speak only for myself and my family. My grandmother has lived as a free woman all her life. She has earned the right to die a free woman. My children were born free and will live free. I will never agree to any proposal that would take their freedom away. To see them settled and safe, I would do whatever it takes. If that means giving up my own freedom, then yes, I would do it."

There was a collective gasp, then the room erupted into whispered conversations among the settlers. They fell to silence as the Jarl began to speak once more.

"Honourable words, my friend. Thank you. Please be seated again. Osric will now explain my proposal in full. It is open to you all, and you are free to accept or reject it. For those who accept, you will have the protection of the king. For those who reject it, you will be given a week to rest here, then you must leave to find your own path, without any formal agreement to protect or provide for you. So think carefully."

Jarl Svend sat down, leaving the floor to Osric.

"This land, like your own," he began, "has suffered much from war and raiders. Many lives have been lost, many families have been bereft. There is a shortage of men and women to work the land and farmsteads are being left to ruin. Jarl Svend's proposal benefits everyone. The head of each household must agree to act as a thrall for two years on an assigned farmstead. The women and children old enough to contribute will be expected to help wherever needed, but not as thralls. They will retain their freedom. In return, you will be guaranteed food and shelter. After two years, your freedom will be returned, and you will be granted land of your own. This will be a formal agreement with your rights protected by the king himself. Everything has a price, you already know that. What you had was won with hard work. This is no different. Work hard and you will win the new life you seek. Brothers Anselm and Colm will take your details and prepare an agreement, which will be signed by both parties and verified by Jarl Svend on behalf of King Olaf. Erik, will you be the first to sign an agreement?"

Erik hesitated only briefly. He had, after all, effectively agreed already. He walked forward and gave his details to Brother Anselm. Brother Colm assigned him to the farmstead of Ælfric and *his wife, Blaedswith, telling him, "The agreement will be ready to sign tomorrow. The farmstead of Ælfric is closer to Jorvik. He will be here tomorrow to sign the agreement and take you and your family to your new home. God go with you."*

As Erik returned to Ravna and the children, others began to make their way forward.

22

Questions and Answers

Freya was running late. She had slept far past her usual time, hanging on to her dream for as long as she could. For the first time it had revealed details that she hoped could be verified. A document had been made formulating the agreement of Erik's enslavement to a man called Ælfric and confirmed under the protection of King Olaf. The farmstead assigned was closer to Jorvik than to Whitby. These were clues that perhaps could prove Erik's existence, so she took the time to jot them down, perhaps to share with Aston or the professor, or maybe she would ask at the record offices in Northallerton and York to do a search.

She felt she was on the brink of something important, but for now she had to hurry to pick Aston up and drive him to visit Connor. As she climbed into the car, she noticed the envelope the professor had given to Aston was still on the back seat. She sighed as she fastened her seatbelt, thinking, "Poor little love. He must have really been upset to have forgotten that." It was puzzling though that he hadn't phoned her to ask about it. Still, it would all sort itself out soon enough when she picked him up.

He was looking out the window as she climbed out of the car. She waved the envelope at him. He disappeared from the window to emerge out of the front door, ignoring the proffered envelope.

"I don't want them until I've spoken to Connor," he said, climbing unceremoniously into the car's front passenger seat. Marie was standing in the doorway and shrugged at Freya. The car horn beeped, and Freya responded, "I'm coming, Aston. Don't be so impatient! I'll see you later, Marie."

Getting back in, Freya threw the envelope into the back. As she fastened her seatbelt and set off, she turned to Aston.

"You do realise Connor may not feel like talking, and we will probably only be allowed to stay a few minutes?"

"But I need to ask him if the printouts in the envelope are really from him," Aston said. "I don't think they are." He looked

Freya in the eye and his honest concern was clear for her to see.

"Why would you think that? The professor clearly said they had been left for you by Connor. Why would he lie?"

A silence followed for a few minutes before Aston let all his concerns run free.

"I don't know why he'd lie, but I don't trust the professor. Connor and I had planned to do the search together. Why would he go ahead without me? He couldn't have known he was going to miss our session because of his accident, and he couldn't have done them afterwards. It makes no sense."

"I see your point, but don't fret about it. If we can't ask Connor, we'll ask the professor himself on Friday. I can't see the harm, though, in us taking a look at what's in the envelope. You don't have to use it in your assignment, and you don't have to agree to publication if you don't want to. The work is your own private property and what happens to it is up to you and you alone. No pressure."

Aston said nothing more than "OK", but his shoulders relaxed, and Freya was content to leave him to his own thoughts for a while, as they hit the motorway.

Aston slipped his hand into Freya's as they entered the ward. Connor was a daunting sight for a small boy. They found him with both legs and his right arm in traction, wired to various machines that beeped intermittently. But he was awake, and glad of their company. He greeted them warmly.

"Hey, partner. Good to see you. How's it going?"

"All good. Are you in a lot of pain?" Aston asked quietly.

"I'm high as a kite on painkillers, but it's a bugger trying to scratch an itch." Connor smiled and pulled a face, making Aston giggle. Then Connor added, "Thanks so much for sorting out my immediate needs, Freya. It was truly kind of you."

"Not a problem, Connor," said Freya. "I would say it was my pleasure, but obviously in the circumstances I wish it hadn't been necessary. Have your parents managed to get to see you?"

"They're coming tomorrow, they've had to sort a few things out on the farm."

"The professor gave me the printouts you left," Aston blurted out. "But I've not had time to look at them yet. I'm sorry."

"Hey, partner, dinnae be fretting yourself. I never left any printouts for you. It was that big guy who left them for you. The one who thinks he's a Viking. Roland, I think his name is. I guess the professor just assumed they were from me."

Aston's face lit up as he looked at Freya, explaining to her as though Connor had been speaking a foreign language that needed an interpreter.

"They're from Rollo, Nan!"

"Well, that explains a lot," she replied with a smile.

They chatted away happily about Aston's progress and Connor's road to recovery, until it was time to leave.

"Time, visitors, please!" a voice rang out.

Freya and Aston took their leave, wishing Connor well and promising to return in a few days, before joining the shuffling queue of visitors leaving the ward.

They enjoyed a nice lunch before they headed home, Aston now eager to see what was in the envelope Rollo had left.

At Marie's house all three gathered around the table as Aston opened the sealed envelope, pulling out a letter from Rollo among the printouts. They read it together, hunched over the A4 piece of printer paper with its hand-scrawled writing.

Hello Aston,
I hope you have been working hard on your assignment. Màné has been focusing her attention on locating real evidence of Erik, who seems to have captured your "imagination" and haunts your Nan's dreams.

"Oh my god, Mother!" Marie exclaimed "You've never mentioned any dreams. I thought you were looking tired. What's been happening?"

Aston gave a whoop.

"I knew he was trying to talk to you, Nan. What did he say?"

Shocked and a little embarrassed that her secret was out in the open, Freya tried to deflect their attention away from it.

"Let's just focus on what Rollo has to say first, shall we?"

The letter continued:

Erik was a common name among the Norse, so it is not possible to say for certain that the documents enclosed relate to the same Erik you are familiar with. The area around or close to the Sentinel was an Anglo-Saxon settlement before it became settled by the Norse. Màné has uncovered a document, a will, which seems to overlap both periods. It is written in Latin, recorded by a local priest from the church of St Æthelflæd (now lost), so I have enclosed a translation with the will.

In essence it is from a man named Ælfric, leaving the land to his faithful friend and former thrall Erik, on the proviso that he continues to allow Ælfric's wife, Blaedswith, to go on living in her own home for the duration of her lifetime. Upon Blaedswith's death, the house is to be given to Freyja, the daughter of Erik. There is more in the translation.

Màné and I hope this helps and is of interest to you.

Kind regards
Rollo

"Oh lord above, he's real! Erik is real and he really did settle at the homestead." It was Freya's turn to exclaim in a shocked voice, though barely above a whisper, as she reached across to grasp Aston's hand.

Marie looked up, saw the shock on her mother's face, and asked, "Is this what you dreamed?"

Freya shook her head.

"Not this part. But last night in my dream, I witnessed the day Erik committed himself to a term of slavery in order to provide his surviving family with a place of safety. The man he was indentured to was called Ælfric, and his wife was Blaedswith. Look, I've made a note of the details so I can have it checked." Freya reached for her bag to retrieve the note she had written that morning, handing it to Marie.

As Marie read her mother's notes her first thought was that it was all some sort of elaborate joke, but in her heart she knew her mother would never trick Aston in such a way,

"You aren't joking are you mum?"

Freya shook her head slowly and Marie went on,

Wow! Ooh, I've gone all shivery, Mum," Marie said. "This is spooky. I take it this isn't the only dream you've had. Màné clearly knows there are more."

"Why didn't you tell me, Nan?" Aston asked, a touch of hurt in his voice.

"I've been having the dreams off and on for some weeks," said Freya apologetically. "Each one picks up from the last and follows Erik's journey from Norway to Whitby and then, it seems, to the homestead, with lots of tragic events in between. I recorded them in a diary and found myself sharing it with Màné. I'm sorry, Aston. I didn't share it with you because, like all good historians, you were working on facts, and I didn't want to confuse you. I thought the dreams were just my imagination. I've got the diary at home. You can read it next time you come."

Aston was shuffling Rollo's letter and the copied documents back into the envelope.

"Let's go to Sentinel Cottage now. We can have tea at yours, then we can read the diary and look at Rollo's stuff."

Marie was reaching for her car keys.

"That sounds like a plan. We'll pick up a take-away on the way to save you cooking, Mum. Come on."

An hour later Marie sat with red-rimmed eyes as she read about Astrid's death and the aftermath of the raid on Erik's village. She covered her mouth with her hand, attempting to stifle the sobs that were threatening to burst forth, looking at Freya through eyes glistening with unshed tears. She could not find her voice to speak or express the sorrow and horror she felt. Freya needed no words. She understood what Marie was feeling, for she had felt it too. Silently, she handed Marie a small brandy and gave her shoulder a comforting squeeze.

"Sometimes when I'm talking to Erik, he gets confused. He thinks I'm Gorm or Ulf, but when I tell him I am Aston, he laughs and says, 'Of course you are.' Aston's bright voice stopped both women in their tracks.

Of course, it wasn't the first time Aston had mentioned Erik but, more often than not, Freya had dismissed it as part of his expanding imagination. This, as far as she could recall, was the first time he had openly spoken about any sort of direct communication.

However, the fleeting image she had experienced, of Aston chatting with someone, during their field walk, flashed across her mind. Marie looked terrified, and with some justification. Freya was forced to admit to herself that she had been remiss in ignoring his past remarks, she knew, however that interrogating him now with frenzied questions would not help in the least. She gave Marie's hand a reassuring squeeze as silently her eyes spoke to Marie 'Leave this to me' they said. She turned her attention back to Aston and calmly responded to his comment. Taking the opportunity to explore Aston's connection with Erik.

"I like Erik. What else does he talk to you about?" she asked, waiting patiently for Aston to respond. He gave a small shrug before he answered

"Lots of things. Sometimes he tells me stories. He calls them Sagas. Or he tries to teach me about sailing or ploughing, mostly when he thinks I am Gorm or Ulf."

"You've often mentioned that he lives in the tree," Freya persisted. "How does that work?"

But if Aston knew the answer, he wasn't telling.

"I don't know. He just does." And he returned his attention back to the diary, snuggling into Marie as they both continued to read.

Time sped by and the take-away had long since been eaten. Freya retreated to make coffee and sandwiches. By the time she returned with the tray, Marie had finished reading the dream diary. They were all glad of the break, and after the spicy take-away, Aston was especially grateful for the chocolate milkshake. Then he was ready to take charge.

"We'll need to establish a timeline for Erik as much as we can and go through the dream diary for clues which we can tie into possible historical sources. The question is, do we do that before we've gone through the rest of the will or after?"

"After!" both Freya and Marie said in unison. And Freya added, "There may be more details in the will to lead to the facts."

Freya passed the envelope to Aston. It had been given to him and he was the owner and author of the work for which it was intended, after all.

The will ran for several pages. Though only a facsimile of the original, it showed the document had been written by a skilled scribe, the copperplate letters occasionally embellished with decorations in coloured ink. As Rollo had pointed out, however, it was written in Latin, which none of them understood, so they turned their attention to the typed translation he had supplied.

This is the last will and testament of Ælfric, son of Osbert, son of Ælfric, son of Osbert, etc. recorded faithfully from the words spoken by the first mentioned Ælfric, (farmer and owner of the land, herein dispersed by law, at the time of King Erik Bloodaxe), to me Osbert, servant of God and priest of the small but holy church of St Æthelflæd.

The words and will of Ælfric, son of Osbert, son of Ælfric and many fathers and sons in an unbroken line from the time of St Cuthbert, all of whom owned and worked the land herein dispersed, by ownership and right of birth. The land herein dispersed, known as the Low Farm, beyond the village of Saxonby, at a place known as the Cross on the Hill, in the Lordship of Jorvik, to the north of the river, stretches east to the crossroads marked by St Æthelflæd's Cross, and follows the boundary of the road to both the north and south for two leagues. To the west, the boundary follows the path of the gill towards the river. To the south of the river, the land stretches north as far as the ancient stones; to the east it matches the boundary already described, as far as the road leading to the village and church of St Æthelflæd and to the west the boundary is the curve of the gill as it joins the river.

Aston broke off, as he shuffled through the papers, and picked out the boundary map Rollo had enclosed.

"We need to compare this with the boundary map David sketched , see if we can locate the extra features that are mentioned."

"Absolutely. It sounds like we'll have a lot to add," said Freya. "But can we finish with the rest of the will first? I'm dying to know more about Erik."

Aston smiled at her. "OK, but remember, patience is a virtue. That's what you always say to me, Nan."

Both Freya and Marie burst into laughter.

"He's got you there, Mum!" Marie chortled.

They huddled together once more, returning their attention to Ælfric's will.

If God had willed it to be so, my land would have passed to my only child, my son Eadred, but it is a cause of sorrow that Eadred was taken from us when the passing army of Danes raided our land, killing my son and stealing what they could to feed their army. May God bless his soul. I have no other family to follow in my steps. It is, therefore, my wish, intent and will that my land passes to Erik the Norseman. He came as a thrall to aid me in working the land in the first year of the reign of King Olaf Guthfrithson and attained his freedom, as agreed, two years later, in the reign of King Olafr Sigtryggson, but he stayed as a freeman to help me work my land to the benefit of us both. He found a home for himself and his family, I found a good and faithful friend. My life is ending, but it would have ended much sooner if it had not been for Erik and his son Gorm, who saved my life when a loaded cart tipped and crushed me beneath it. Together they pulled me free and carried me home. They did not shirk their work when I was recovering, but both worked twice as hard, to provide for me and my wife, Blaedswith. My land is therefore to pass to Erik, and after him to his son Gorm, providing my wife, Blaedswith, is allowed to continue living in the home she has known and cared for over many years. Upon her death the house is to pass to Erik's daughter, Freyja, for the child has become like a daughter to us. This is my will and I entrust its execution to be overseen by the good priest Osbert of our church of St Æthelflæd.

Signed with the mark of Ælfric X

Written in the reign of King Erik Bloodaxe

Witnessed by me, Osbert, above described,
and by the Jarl Sigmund, as the representative of King
Erik Bloodaxe

"Oh! Wow! Wow! Wow! It has everything you need to finish your assignment, Aston. It tells us so much about those who owned the land under the Saxons and how it became a Norse settlement. We should raise a toast to Rollo and Màné for finding it and sending it to you." Freya was almost bouncing up and down on her chair with excitement.

"It's getting late, so I'll raise a cup of coffee since I have to drive back home," Marie responded.

Surprisingly Aston looked a bit down in the dumps. Both Freya and Marie thought he was just getting overtired, until he spoke.

"I don't think Erik planted the Sentinel. If it was shown on the boundary document of 946, it must have already been established long enough for it to be noteworthy. I'll have to check the dates, but I think King Olaf Guthfrithson died in 941, Erik Bloodaxe ruled briefly in 948 but was expelled in 949 when Olafr Sigtryggson succeeded. Erik Bloodaxe had a second reign from 952. If Erik succeeded to the land under Bloodaxe, in either of his reigns, he could not have been responsible for planting a tree already of significant size in 946. Does that make sense?"

It made perfect sense, and Freya was also deflated. It was Marie who rallied them by pointing out, "Doesn't that make the Sentinel even more significant? If it pre-dates the Norse settlement, it could well date much further back to the Druids. The will says Ælfric's family held the land from the time of St Cuthbert. Presumably he was doing missionary work and converting pagans. The Druids set great store by oak trees."

Reluctantly Freya had to concur.

"You're right, of course. But we've got so used to thinking of it as dating from the Norse period, and Erik in particular, it's almost like finding out you never really knew an old and valued friend."

"Oh, come on, Mum. That's a bit dramatic. Anyway, it was the Sentinel that drew you here, long before you knew anything about the Norse settlement and Erik in particular."

142

That gave Freya pause for thought. Aston was keeping his thoughts to himself and remained silent. He only knew that the will forced him to re-evaluate all his theories about the Norse settlement and would mean a lot of rewriting of his assignment, which was now due in less than a week. Furthermore, he had his final session with the professor tomorrow and he had added nothing to his work since his last one. A little later, as they were preparing to leave, he asked Marie, in a pleading tone,

"Mum, can I stay up and work on my assignment? I have to download the will and do a bit more work so it's ready for the professor tomorrow."

Marie was adamant in her refusal.

"Absolutely not. It's already close to midnight and you've had a long day. If the professor isn't happy, it's tough. You're not working for him. This is your own work, and you can work at your own pace until you go back to school."

Freya knew her daughter was right, but even so, she sympathised with the crestfallen look on Aston's face.

"Don't worry about tomorrow. Just use the time to talk things through with the professor, use him as a sounding board. He won't mind and I think he'll be very interested. Get a good night's sleep and I'll see you tomorrow." She gave Aston a kiss and hugged Marie, before watching them drive off.

The wind was getting up, whispering through the leaves of the Sentinel.

"What other secrets will you reveal to us?" she murmured, looking across to the mighty oak. Then she whispered, "Goodnight, Erik. I'm glad you're a part of our lives and our journey. I ask one thing of you – Please bring no harm to Aston, Bless him with your protection"

If she was expecting a mystical response, none came. She went inside and prepared for bed, making sure Fen and Arty were comfortable for the night. No dreams came.

23

An Extraordinary Ordinary Day

The morning dawned, sunny but blustery, with leaves being blown everywhere as Freya and her wolves walked around the boundary of Lucky's Grove. Fen and Arty were in high spirits, having had only a cursory walk to the river and back the evening before. They expended their excess energy chasing and jumping to catch the falling leaves, making Freya laugh. Making up for their restricted exercise the evening before, she took them on a second circuit of the grove before leading them home. Their tongues lolling, they looked as though they were smiling. She looked at them with pride and, she suddenly realised, with love. She had never owned a pet of any sort before, but she had taken on the care of the wolves with true commitment to their welfare, which bound them together. She had been unprepared for the emotional bond that had developed between them.

Calling them to heel so they could enter the garage in the correct pack order, she rewarded their obedience with a dazzling smile.

"My beautiful boys. I'm so lucky to have you."

Giving them extra attention as she groomed them, she finally settled them down after giving them their breakfast. As she locked the door of their pen, she promised them, "After today, I won't have to disappear so much, so we can spend more time outside."

Her early morning walk, and an undisturbed sleep, had given her a good appetite. Before Aston arrived, she prepared a good (not very healthy) breakfast. She was ready to dish it up as he ran in.

"Mum's gone straight to work and will pick me up about six o'clock," he announced as he sat at the table in the dining room, filling his bowl with cereal at the same time.

"Okey doke," replied Freya. "I need to stop at the solicitors in Ripon to exchange contracts on the land before we go to see the professor. I hope you don't mind."

"No, that's cool. Will it really be ours then?"

"Absolutely. More protection for the Sentinel."

Aston raised his glass of orange juice. "To the Sentinel and Erik."

Freya raised her cup of coffee to chink it against Aston's glass, repeating the toast.

Much later they emerged from the professor's office with Aston feeling more confident, all his concerns put to rest. The professor had congratulated him on his assessment of the dating evidence on the Sentinel, confirming the tree must have been planted prior to the Norse settlement. The Professor, leaned across his desk, holding Aston's gaze,

"Be assured that this in no way alters the fact that a Norse settlement had existed, and the importance of it remains the same. The inclusion of the will is exactly the sort of evidence I had hoped for, a contemporary source that has never been used before. Don't underestimate its importance Aston. It proves when the transition of the land from Saxon to Norse took place."

Aston mentioned his intention to rewrite the entire assignment in light of the will, the professor shook his head,

"At this stage it is neither a wise nor a necessary action to take. You should just amend some of the introductory and leading sentences to accommodate the Saxon connection. Any re-writes or further editing will come much further down the line, during the publication process."

Astone beamed in relief, Freya picked up the question of publication,

"So what sort of time-scale for publication are we looking at Citric? Christmas or New Year perhaps?"

"I'm sorry to disappoint you both, but the publication of n academic work is a slow process. There will be peer reviews, re-writes, professional editing, followed by the production and printing process. A period of at least two years is more realistic I'm afraid."

Freya swallowed her disappointment, giving Aston's hand a comforting squeeze, as they thanked the professor for all his help.

"It been a pleasure getting to know you both, and of course this is not the end our association. The start of a new academic year is a busy period for student and tutor alike, but I will be in touch in due course. You have a few changes to make but you have nothing to worry about Aston."

Making their way from the university, Freya asked Aston how he felt about the publication being delayed by such a considerable time and was surprised by his response.

"I'm glad, Nan. I don't really want it published at all. It's our project about our land, but if it was published, it would belong to everyone and I don't want that."

"It's your choice," she replied. "But I think you have to tell the professor."

They called into WH Smith's. Freya intended to buy some magazines for Connor, but Aston pointed out that perhaps an Amazon gift card would be better so he could download music or talking books to listen to on headphones. Since Connor only had one arm free from traction, it was a sensible choice. Purchases made, they headed to the hospital.

Reporting to the nurses' station, they were informed that Connor's mother was with him and, as visitors were restricted to only two at a time, only one of them could go in. Freya turned to Aston.

"It should be you. Are you confident enough to go in without me? I'll wait here."

With only slight reluctance and a nod of encouragement from Freya, Aston agreed. He had barely vanished beyond the ward door when a fraught-looking woman emerged, of medium height and solid build. She caught Freya's eye.

"Are you Aston's granny?" she asked hesitantly. Her Scottish accent gave away her identity.

"Yes," said Freya. "You must be Connor's mother. I'm pleased to meet you, and I apologise for our intrusion"

"Call me Hannah. And no apologies needed. I wanted to thank you for the kindness you have shown to Connor. It was difficult for us to get away immediately, I'm so glad you were here for him."

Freya assured Hannah no thanks were needed as they shook hands.

"Connor has told me so much about Aston," Hannah continued. "You must be enormously proud of him. I'm sure they will have lots to talk about. Shall we leave them to it and grab a cup of coffee? I could certainly use one."

Sitting in the hospital café, nursing her coffee, Freya asked Hannah about Connor's prognosis.

"Och! It may not look like it, but he was lucky. There are no complications. It will take time, but he will make a full recovery. Once his fractures are healed and he can come off traction, he'll need rehabilitation, which could take months. But the important thing is he will recover. He could have been killed and I don't know how we would have coped with that. To lose a child is unthinkable."

Freya agreed. Rooting in her handbag, she pulled out a pen, and scribbled her phone number on a napkin.

"If you need anything, don't hesitate to call me. And I mean it."

The conversation moved on to Hannah sharing memories of Connor's childhood. He had grown up on his family's farm in an isolated area of the Scottish Highlands. Exploring the rich history of the area with his father had sparked his love of history and archaeology. Choosing to pursue his interest at university was a natural progression.

"Though his father hoped he would stay on the farm, we are both so proud of his achievement." Hannah beamed, before adding, "Your Aston has a very bright future ahead of him, too, I'm told. A published academic work at such a young age is a fantastic accomplishment."

Freya smiled and nodded. But, conscious that Aston had not told the professor yet of his reluctance to publish his work, she refrained from sharing this with Hannah. She glanced at her watch.

"We better get back. Visiting hour is almost over."

They arrived back on the ward just in time. Freya took her leave.

"It was so nice to meet you, Hannah. Please do call if you need anything at all. Aston is back in school on Monday, but we will come again next Saturday if that's OK. Please give my best wishes to Connor."

"I will, I promise." Hannah did not prolong her goodbye as the nurse was chivvying visitors off the premises. Hannah, of course, had permission to stay and returned quickly to Connor's side.

Excited by his conversation with Connor, Aston declined a meal in York, wanting to get back to Freya's to work on his assignment. So they bought sandwiches, crisps and drinks in the hospital shop to snack on as they made their way home.

As Aston worked on the various boundary maps they now had, Freya exercised Fen and Arty before preparing the evening meal, a chicken, spinach, and pasta bake. Once it was in the oven, she went to check on Aston's progress.

"Have you any tracing paper, Nan? If I trace each of the maps and superimpose each image on to the others, it may be easier to see the connections."

"Let me check, and while I'm looking, it may be a good time for you to telephone Rollo to thank him for finding and sending the will."

"I've already done it, first thing this morning. He was pleased it helped."

Freya handed him the pad of tracing paper she had found in the bureau.

"Shall I do one for you to save time?" she asked.

Aston was only too willing to accept. Soon they were both absorbed in their task and a clearer picture of the extent of Ælfric's legacy to Erik emerged. The problem was none of the maps had been drawn to scale, and neither Aston nor Freya had any idea of how a league was measured in terms of miles. Looking at the latest boundary map, Freya was forced to point out another item of interest.

"I've just realised, in the months I've been living here, I've never travelled east of the road beyond my own cottage. It looks like we have some exploring to do tomorrow. What do you think, Aston?"

"Can we? Do you think David would have one of those wheelie things that take measurements that we could borrow?" he asked enthusiastically.

"A wheelie thing that takes measurements? I'm not sure I know what you mean."

Aston tutted in frustration.

"Yes, you do, Nan. It's like the line markers they used to mark out the football pitch in my old school, only as it's pushed along it records the distance travelled. If we got the measurements, we could scale the boundary maps."

"I'm with you. I'll ask him. If he's free, he might like to join us." Freya reached for her phone as she spoke, scrolling to David's number and giving a tap.

The conversation was brief but successful. She smiled as she hung up, turning once more to Aston.

"David has exactly what we need and will be joining our quest."

"Yes!" Aston pumped the air with a raised fist.

The timer on the cooker pinged, just as a car horn sounded outside.

"That will be your mum, just nicely timed. I think we've done all we can for today, so if you tidy away your things and set the table, I'll go and check our tea."

In the kitchen Freya listened to Aston excitedly telling Marie all about their day and their plans for tomorrow. Marie was genuinely pleased that the professor had been so helpful. She was also keen to hear about the planned search tomorrow. The revelation about Freya's dreams had edged her interest from supportive onlooker to engaged participant.

"The search sounds really exciting. Can I come too?" she asked Freya over tea.

"Of course. But I thought you were working."

"Oh, I swapped my shift so I could see Peter. He won't mind tagging along."

"The more the merrier. This is turning into quite an expedition." Freya smiled over at Aston.

"Mum can be the emergency driver in case all that walking gets too much for you or David," Aston said.

"What a good idea to have the oldies covered," Freya shot back, only a hint of acidic humour in her tone.

It wasn't lost on Marie. She laughed as she reached to touch Freya's hand.

"It's a sensible precaution only. Better safe than sorry. We don't know how far we'll have to walk."

.

149

24

New Discoveries

It was a sizeable group that set out the following morning. Peter had brought an Ordnance Survey map of the area and walked ahead to scout out the terrain. Aston walked slightly behind him, pushing the measuring wheel. He stopped every now and again as they came to a significant "landmark" (Freya's front garden, the two fields and Lucky's Grove included, adding others along the way), noting the individual measurement of each before moving on. David took endless photographs in the hope that they could match up the contours of the horizon with the boundary maps. Freya interchanged her position, sometimes walking behind David, sometimes by his side or hurrying ahead to walk with Aston., but always with a keen eye to spot anything significant. Marie, in the car, drove slowly behind, in the centre of the road, to force the occasional traffic to slow down and give way to the walking party. They looked like an official, well-organised walking group. Who would have thought they had organised themselves only as they left Sentinel Cottage?

Freya's land, on the opposite side to the Sentinel and running east to Lucky's Grove, was relatively flat. Just beyond the grove, however, the road descended into a valley, the landscape changing gradually from gentle hills and dales to the more rugged, wilder landscape of the moors. Freya had the same feeling she had felt when she had stepped out of the patio doors into the garden of Sentinel Cottage for the first time, as though she had entered another world. She slipped her hand into David's, unsure whether she wanted to share the moment with him or just needed to keep a grip on reality.

At the base of the hill, the road evened out for about a mile before it rose steeply again. Marie pulled the car into a layby just before they hit the rise and climbed out.

"Aston, are you OK to keep going or do you want a ride?"

"I'm fine, Mum." Aston's response was swift.

"What about you, Mum? I'm no good on hill starts, so now's the time to get in if you don't fancy walking all the way up that steep hill."

Freya hesitated, until David urged her to accept.

"Come on, we've earned it, and we'll be fresher when the search starts for real."

As they walked together to the car, Marie stepped aside.

"You drive, Mum, and I'll walk behind Aston. Don't worry about being the rear-guard. Just drive straight on to get up the hill and stop where you can, either at the top or at the bottom. Do you want me to take over as photographer, David?"

David handed her the camera without a word and Marie ran to catch up with Aston, waving as Freya and David drove past. Just for a moment, as they crested the hill, Freya was certain she saw a tall Saxon cross on the summit of the hill, but when she looked again, she realised it was a stunted, windblown tree.

As they descended the incline, the road flattened once more for a few hundred yards before it became the feed for a T-junction. On the opposite side of the junction was a layby, where Freya parked to wait for the walkers to catch up. While they waited, she and David raided the snack box and helped themselves to a cup of tea from the thermos and a sandwich. For a while they sat in companionable silence, enjoying the view of the wild moorland.

"He's a remarkable boy, your Aston. He deserves so much recognition for his dedication. I hope that professor doesn't let him down and keeps his promise to publish his work."

David's remark was triggered by the sight of the walkers cresting the hill and starting the descent, Aston still pushing the mile counter. Freya sighed before answering.

"I think the professor is more than willing to keep his promise. The problem is Aston has decided he doesn't want to publish it."

"What? It's an incredible opportunity for him, one that could influence his whole future. Have you told him that?" David was shocked, the more so when he heard Freya's reply.

"No. I've told him it's his decision. It's worrying me, though, because I know you're right. I haven't discussed it with Marie yet, so we'll see what she thinks. In the meantime, keep it to yourself, please."

David grunted, before adding, after a pause, "Don't sit on it too long. She needs to know, and the lad needs sound advice."

"Yes, I know." Freya's retort was clipped, but she refrained from saying more as Peter, Aston and Marie were about to cross the road to join them.

As the three new arrivals sprawled on the grass verge exploring the selections in the snack box, Peter passed the OS map to Aston.

"I think the first part of your quest is complete. That large hill with the tree on top is called Cross Hill, and this road is marked as being the Cross Road. That ties in with the will, doesn't it?"

Aston agreed, pleasure showing in his smile as he studied the map. They were all equally delighted. Marie made Aston pose for a photograph with the hill and road as the backdrop.

"The OS map doesn't happen to show the location for the lost village and church, does it?" Freya asked hopefully.

Peter and Aston scanned the map carefully, but could see no sign of either, other than the fact that a field (one included in Freya's new acquisitions) bore the name Chapel Field. However, its location didn't match information given in the will.

"Nope, I'm afraid not." Peter shook his head.

"We'll just have to carry on looking. We may find ruins." Aston was so enthusiastic he was already picking up the mile counter.

As they were all sufficiently rested, they prepared to continue the search. Marie packed away the snack box and collected the rubbish into a large paper bag, which she stashed in the boot. They left the car where it was and set off, more or less in the order they had begun the day, heading south.

Ælfric's will had placed the eastern boundary as running for two leagues north to south, so they calculated a total distance of six miles all together. For ease of reference, they divided this into three miles each way. They had not expected to find either the village or the church in any recognisable form, but they did hope to find some remnant to indicate they had existed.

After covering the three miles south, they had found nothing but open moorland. They were all disappointed, none more so than Aston, who urged them keep looking and go on for one more mile. No one had the heart to deny him, so on they went, but all they found was a flock of moorland sheep, trying to get the better of the sheepdog, despite his determination to round them up and move them into a pen. The farmer waited patiently for his dog to complete the task successfully. Only then did Freya make her move. Waving her arms to attract the farmer's attention, she made her way quickly towards the sheep, with Aston following closed behind. Seeing them, the farmer assumed they were another bunch of lost hikers. He drove towards them, stopping as he came to Freya, still waving her arms.

"Lost, are you? Aye, well you're not the first and won't be the last, I reckon. There's a footpath on the other side of the road. Follow that and you'll soon be in the village."

Freya thanked him but quickly put him in the picture.

"We're actually looking for any sign of an ancient church and village that was around here. My grandson is doing some research into the local area for a school assignment. I don't suppose you could help us, by any chance."

"You won't find any actual remains," replied the farmer. "The buildings were all made of wood back then, more than a thousand years ago, and will have long since rotted. Follow the path into the village and talk to the vicar there. The village organised an event to mark some centenary or other a few years ago and got specialists in to search with radar or something. I don't know what they found, but Stanley Williams will be happy to help you. Good luck with the project, young man."

Freya thanked him most sincerely, as did Aston, who was hopping around excitedly.

"Can we go there now, Nan? Please?"

"Yes, if you stop hopping around me like a boxing kangaroo."

The helpful farmer laughed, waving them on their way, and they headed back to the road to re-join the others. Peter checked the OS map and located the footpath leading to the village of Nurham,

"Shouldn't take us long. It's about a mile and a half. Last there buys the tea and cakes."

It was a lovely little village, very typical of most of those found in the Yorkshire Dales, with one road in and out. A scattering of cottages nestled around the village green, with an ancient oak at the centre. There was a shop and a pub, and just on the edge of the village stood the church, dedicated to St Mary.

It was market day, so the church was open to serve market goers with beverages and snacks. Afternoon tea was at a special discount. Soon the trestle table occupied by Freya, Marie, David and Aston was brimming over with homemade fare, courtesy of Peter, who had been the last to enter the church and consequently fell foul of his own rule. He took his seat after placing the order.

"The vicar is on tea duty," he told them. "So I suggest we tuck in before we approach him for information."

They were glad to do just that, munching their way through cucumber and crème fraiche sandwiches, and an array of small cakes and scones with homemade strawberry jam and cream. It was delightful. Then, as it happened, the vicar made it his business to approach them.

"Beautiful afternoon to explore the Dales. Are you on holiday?"

Freya quickly filled him in on their residential status and explained how they had found their way to Nurham to speak to him.

"My grandson is researching the history of the area for a school project. We were advised that you could help with information on the lost village of Saxonby and the Saxon church dedicated to St Æthelflæd."

The vicar was delighted.

"Call me Stan. Come with me, young man. There is an exhibition of our eight-hundredth anniversary, with lots of information and booklets telling the story of the old village and church, plus a DVD of the archaeology undertaken at the time."

Aston practically leapt up from his seat. Freya wasn't far behind.

"Do you mind if I come too, Stan? Aston's enthusiasm has rubbed off and I find myself fascinated."

"By all means. You are most welcome. It's a public exhibition, so you are all free to explore it at your leisure." Stan's latter remark was aimed at the remaining members of the party. They nodded their appreciation, though it seemed they were quite content to carry on tucking into the remainder of their afternoon tea.

Stan led Freya and Aston from the church hall into the nave of the church, where they found several noticeboards filled with photographs. The first showed a group of people in medieval costume, presumably residents of Nurham, gathered outside the church door. Stan explained its significance.

"Our church was built in the thirteenth century, with the foundation stone laid in 1218, so we felt it would be significant to mark the eight hundredth anniversary by focusing on the time of its foundation, hence the costumes. This church replaced a smaller, wattle and daub structure."

Other photographs showed the villagers re-enacting various aspects of medieval life such as archery, carpentry, dyeing cloth and cooking. They were of particular interest to Aston.

"I'm a re-enactor too. I like learning about the way people lived in the past," he told Stan, earning himself some brownie points,

"Are you really? How fascinating. What period do you re-enact?" Stan asked.

"Viking. My Nan's land was part of a Saxon, then Norse settlement. It's not far from here." Aston was at his chattering best, fired by excitement.

"Come and look at the aerial photographs," said Stan. "The site of the ancient village and church is marked in red. You may be able to relate the location to your Nan's land, if it's close by." Stan's own excitement was growing, as he led them to a second noticeboard holding a large, blown-up aerial photograph.

Freya and Aston looked carefully at it. The T-junction was clearly visible. The site of the lost church was shown to be about a mile and a half along the southern arm of the T, with the village not directly opposite but a few hundred yards to the south, on the other side of the road. Following the line of the main road, Lucky's Grove was clearly visible.

Aston pointed it out.

"There! That's Lucky's Grove. It forms the current boundary to my Nan's land, though the original settlement was bigger and ran close to the lost church. That's why we were looking for it today, to trace the original boundary."

"Fascinating! What led you to that conclusion?" Stan asked, clearly interested in following a new source.

"We have a will from a Saxon called Ælfric," explained Freya. "He left his land to Erik, who was a Viking, so it marked the

155

change of ownership from Saxon to Norse. The will describes the boundary of the land owned by Ælfric, all of which became Erik's. It was recorded by the priest of the lost church."

"How exciting. Do you think I could take a look at it sometime?" Stan asked, politely enough, though the look in his eyes was almost pleading.

Aston nodded, "Sure," he said, then added his own question, "If the church and village were lost, and no remains showed above the ground, how did you find them?"

"Well, it wasn't easy, Aston, and I suppose we got lucky. Although we had no written records, local legend is full of stories about the lost village, which we collected. Then we found a reference to the haunted village in the local archives, which added that the village had been stricken by pestilence and all but a few of the inhabitants died. People were very superstitious at that time. It was noted that many of those who seemed to die, in fact came back to life a few hours later. Now, we would understand that perhaps they had simply slipped into unconsciousness for a while, but they were said to be the living dead, like vampires." Stan hesitated, conscious that the rest of the story was not strictly suitable for children. He diverted attention away from the myths surrounding the village to the archaeology they had undertaken. He led Aston to the third and final noticeboard, filled with photographs. There were lots showing people walking in line across the width of the fields and some of people using metal detectors.

"Collectively, the community spent many hours walking the fields. We found nothing of significance in the fields furthest away, but as we moved closer to the road and footpath, we found a few artefacts that had been turned up by ploughing. The broken sherds of pottery we were unable to get a definitive date for, but we did find a number of knives and an iron cooking pot, which we were able to date to the later Saxon period." He pointed at the photographs of the finds.

"They're like the things they found at Coppergate in York, aren't they, Nan?"

Freya agreed, adding, "The Coppergate finds were confirmed to be from the Viking period, but I suppose there was a fine line which overlaps both Saxon and Norse occupation."

"Absolutely. There are many instances where both the Saxon and Norse communities intermingled," said Stan. "And in many cases the Norse converted to Christianity, so the lost church may well have had a mixed congregation." Then he turned back to the photographs.

"After we started finding solid evidence of occupation, we got a group of detectorists in to go over the field. Regrettably, they didn't turn up either a Saxon or Norse hoard, although they did find a rather beautiful brooch and several lumps of what is termed, slag, the remains or waste product of ironworking. So that was more evidence of human occupation of the site."

"What happened to the finds?" Aston asked, looking at the blurry images of what seemed like an array of muddy, rusty bits and pieces.

"Oh, they went to the museum, of course, although they weren't interested in the slag. That's on the table by the vestry. The finds encouraged us to go a step further." He pointed to a photograph of a rather scruffy-looking man, walking the field with some sort of machine.

"I know what that is," Aston announced. "It's ground-penetrating radar, isn't it?"

"You're a very well-informed young man," Stan said. "But GPR proved too expensive for us to use, and we were advised that it probably wasn't our best option anyway. What you're looking at is a magnetometer. It's less expensive to use, and we were lucky enough to have a member of our congregation who belonged to a local group that had its own machine. She made the arrangements with her group so we could make use of their expertise at a reasonable rate, so that's what we used. That was how we located the actual site of the church and village. It took some time, but we did it." Stan was rightly proud of their achievements.

Aston was impressed.

"How does it work?" he asked.

"Ah, as I understand it, the magnetometer picks up changes in the soil from infilled cuts, such as ditches, waste pits or burnt-out remains of timber, owing to different magnetic fields. Bear in mind, though, that I am not an expert and this is a very simplified version of the process, I'm sure."

Freya had wandered over to the table holding a selection of booklets about the lost village and church, and the archaeological search for their location. She had gathered most of them up when Aston and Stan approached. She handed her hoard to Stan.

"I'll take these. Did you say you had a DVD available too?"

Stan scrabbled under the table and brought out to two copies of the DVD. One he placed on the table, the other he handed to Freya with her selection of books.

"We'll call that £20 all in," he smiled.

"Thank you so much for your time," Freya said, handing him the cash. "I didn't hold out much hope of us finding anything when we set out this morning, but this has been amazing."

Aston also thanked Stan for his help. The vicar beamed.

"Come back anytime, Aston. And if you have any questions, my number is in the books. It's been a pleasure sharing our little exhibition with you."

It was early evening when they arrived back at Sentinel Cottage. They had spent time wandering around the market before heading back to the car. Aston had been focused on the two tasks he had set himself: not only to look for the lost village and church, but also to measure the land to draw up a scaled sketch of the three boundary maps and amalgamate them into one, so they had much more walking to do. He had collected a huge amount of data, including photographs, for the north, south, east and west of the boundaries by the time they were done. Finally, happy but tired from their walk, they elected to eat out to celebrate the success of their day of discovery.

25

Sharing is Caring

Sunday marked the last day of the summer holidays. As usual when Marie didn't have to work, Freya was invited to Sunday lunch. Aston was busy with editing and adding all the new information to his assignment, so Freya took the opportunity to tell Marie of his decision not to publish it.

Marie was unflummoxed.

"If the professor thinks it should be published, then it will be published. But don't worry, Mum, I won't force Aston into doing it." She smiled. "A bit of gentle psychology will guide him into making the decision for himself. Leave it with me. Just follow my lead over lunch."

As they gathered around the table, Aston enthusiastically updated them on his assignment.

"All that information Stan gave us is brilliant. It just rounds it all off nicely, and it's original research too."

Marie was quick to take her opening.

"Oh, it's amazing how we stumbled across it. Just think, if Stan and the villagers had kept their findings to themselves, the lost village and church would have remained lost, and we would know nothing about it."

Freya picked up Marie's line of thought.

"I really enjoyed looking around the exhibition. So kind and thoughtful of them to share such special memories. Did you find the booklets helpful, Aston?"

"They're really cool, Nan. Thanks for buying them for me. Do you remember Stan telling us about the villagers who died and came back to life?" Seeing Freya's nod, he went on. "Do you know what happened to them?" It was a rhetorical question which Aston answered himself. "Everyone was so frightened, thinking they were vampires or possessed by the Devil, so the priest and the survivors killed them, cut their heads off and removed their hearts. Then they buried them outside the church grounds, binding their souls with magic so they couldn't rise again."

"Goodness! That's very gruesome. But how did Stan and his friends know that? They only tested the ground with magnetometry. They never actually dug up any remains, did they?"

"No, but they found an original document. A report written by the priest of the church to his bishop which gave all the details. It's awesome, isn't it?"

"It amazes me," said Marie, "that they could do all that work and share it so unselfishly, so others, like you, Aston, could learn from it and use it in their own work. It takes very special people to do that, I believe."

After lunch they watched the DVD of the scruffy-looking man using the magnetometer. It was very amateurish, opening with a wobbly image of the man, who introduced himself as Tony Hobson before explaining how the equipment worked. Held about twenty centimetres above the ground. the probes picked up magnetic signals from the soil. Solid objects would show up as denser areas, which they called anomalies, and they could prove useful to trace buildings or walls buried underground. There followed a lot of footage of Tony, wielding the equipment, walking the fields in straight lines. Finally, the scene changed to the church hall as Tony revealed his finding to the villagers. Two slides followed, both greyscale images, somewhat blurred, that showed a series of black marks. Those on the first image seemed to be spread around a clear inner circle. The second image also showed a series of black marks, this time, however, appearing to form a vague rectangular shape. Tony then presented his findings individually. He summarised that the first image was of a series of post holes, representing a collection of buildings arranged around the inner circle. This he felt could well represent the traditional grouping of a medieval village around a village green. The second image showed a single building, but there were indications of burials beyond the building itself. It would be relatively safe to say this was the church and graveyard, though without further archaeological investigation, the evidence could not be considered conclusive.

Marie flicked the DVD off with an air of disappointment. Aston sighed.

"So, it may not be the village and church after all."

"I think it's likely," Freya countered. "After all, it fits with the description in Ælfric's will. But Tony and Stan didn't have the

160

benefit of that information, so they had to be careful in their conclusions."

Not saying anything else, Aston retired back to his room to finish off his assignment.

Freya looked at Marie.

"So, what now?" she asked. Marie winked at her.

"Now we have a cup of coffee and wait."

Freya was getting ready to leave when Aston came running down the stairs.

"I hope you don't mind, Nan. I know I said I wanted to keep the assignment just for us, apart from the school that is, but I've been thinking, Stan did a good thing sharing their findings with others, so I've decided to agree to my work being published. Is that OK?"

Freya hugged him.

"It's more than OK. I think it's wonderful."

Marie hugged him too.

"I think it's wonderful too. Well done you."

Marie walked Freya to the car as Aston vanished back to his room.

"I told you," she laughed. "Dangle the right carrot and the donkey will follow where you want it to go."

Freya joined in her mirth, asking, "How did you become so clever, wise and devious?"

"I learned from the best!" Marie gave Freya a kiss before waving her off.

26

The Fall of a Villain

Monday morning dawned. For Aston it was his first day back at school and submission day for his assignment. He had sent the completed file over to Freya late the previous night, making her the proudest Nan in the kingdom. It was wonderful. Despite this, her nerves were on edge. She had received a positive response to her complaint about Miss Carey's intention to ban Aston from submitting his work, assuring her that Aston would be included in the assessment. Nevertheless, she was worried that Miss Carey would not respond in the same way and some negativity would be aimed at Aston. She hated the thought.

Marie dropped him at school on her way to work, but Freya was to pick him up after school. It was a long day with Freya unable to settle to anything.

As the clock crept towards three o'clock, she drove to the school and was parked outside ten minutes early. When Aston finally arrived, he was bright and breezy, flinging his school bag on to the back seat as he climbed into the car next to Freya.

"Hi, Nan. What's for tea?" This was his usual greeting.

"Gosh, I haven't given tea a thought yet. Shall we go to the drive thru and get a take-away to tide us over?" This was Freya's usual response.

Ten minutes later, as Aston tucked into a cheeseburger, Freya was able to check on his school day.

"It was fine," he replied. "We had to hand our assignments into the office. They're going to be marked by the Head, who will act as an independent assessor."

"That's good news. How was Miss Carey with you?"

"She won't be a problem anymore, we've got a new form teacher this year and all our lessons were with different teachers."

"Good. But if she's ever iffy with you again, you let me know. You have ketchup on your nose, by the way."

When Marie arrived much later to collect Aston, she had news that finally settled Freya's concerns.

"Sorry, I intended to let you know sooner, but work has been hectic today. Miss Carey won't be discriminating against any child from now on. She's on a warning of instant dismissal for unprofessional conduct."

"I'll drink to that!" Freya raised her cup of coffee, looking forward to living without any more drama and a less frantic schedule.

27

Colonel Winguard's Secret

The letter arrived as October moved into its third quarter. Freya picked it up from the mat inside the front porch, glancing at the franked postmark as she carried it to the kitchen. It was marked "Evening-tide Nursing Home". She dropped it on the table, thinking, "Don't tell me Daniel is planning on putting me in a nursing home now!"

She finished making her breakfast, then read the letter as she sipped her coffee. She was surprised to see it was from Colonel Winguard, who had sold her Sentinel Cottage. It was brief and to the point. The colonel simply requested that she visit him to discuss matters beneficial to them both and to the Sentinel. It intrigued her enough for her to telephone the nursing home straight away to arrange the visit.

Colonel Winguard sat in a comfortable armchair placed by the tall window of his room. Once he had stood tall, commanding and authoritative. Now he was thin, shrunken and frail. A tartan rug covered his knees. As Freya entered the room, he went to stand up, but she urged him not to, as she hurried across the room to shake his hand.

"Please don't get up on my account, Colonel Winguard. I'm pleased to meet you at last."

"Thank you for making the time to see me so quickly, Ms Fraser. Please be seated. We have much to talk about and time is no longer in my favour."

Freya sat in the chair opposite the colonel. She felt a little awkward, aware that she should have made a point of visiting him much sooner. He had shown her much kindness in negotiating the terms of her purchase of Sentinel Cottage. Once she was settled, he smiled at her.

"How are you finding life in Sentinel Cottage, Ms Fraser?"

"Wonderful. My life is wonderful now. I feel like I was meant to be there. Thank you for your generosity in selling it to me."

"What do you know about the Norns?"

The colonel's question seemed random. Freya looked at him puzzled.

"Nothing. I've never heard of them. Are they people or a geographical feature?" she asked, in all seriousness.

Colonel Winguard did not laugh at her ignorance but apologised instead.

"Forgive me. It was an unfair question. In Norse mythology, the Norns are three sisters. They sit at the base of Yggdrasil, the tree of life, and there they spin and weave together the threads of each person's life, leaving nothing to chance. Where one person's life touches another, it is because the Norns decreed it would be so. They are experts at what they do. Often, they weave together the threads of several lives, and their designs are intricate and complex. There is no such thing as coincidence or luck." The colonel stopped speaking and waited, seeing the beginnings of understanding in Freya's eyes.

She had debated this so many times with herself, thinking of the first time she had set eyes on the Sentinel and her immediate reaction. Her first meeting with David, and the circumstances of her viewing and buying Sentinel Cottage. She had concluded for herself that somehow it was far more than chance. She was sure that fate had had a hand in that and all that followed. Yet she was not ready to admit or accept it without question just yet.

The colonel seemed to follow her unspoken thoughts.

"Tell me about the journey which led you to the Sentinel. Why were you travelling on that road? Was it a planned journey to a known destination? Did you veer off your route and get lost? An impulse perhaps? Which?"

Freya closed her eyes for a moment, immediately transported back to the day she received the letter about her lottery win.

"The catalyst was a letter," she told him. "It was good news, news that most people live in hope of receiving. But it frightened me. I couldn't let myself believe it. I thought it was most likely a hoax and I couldn't bear to see all my hopes come crashing down and the despair that would bring. I couldn't think beyond that. I don't actually remember getting in the car or where I had driven."

A nurse interrupted, entering the room to give the colonel some pills, but left quickly, seeing the annoyance at the interruption.

165

"Please go on, Ms Fraser," the colonel urged and Freya continued.

"I pulled into a garage somewhere because the petrol light was flashing, and then drove on, more by instinct than anything else. I was feeling calmer by then. The need to concentrate on driving, on discovering where I was, made me focus. Everything else, especially the letter, was pushed to the back of my mind. When I came to a crossroad, there was a road sign directing the traffic flow towards Masham. I knew Masham. We had holidayed close by years ago. But I didn't drive that way. I took the opposite route, signposted to the Sign of the Two Wolves. I assumed it was an inn of some sort and I needed a comfort break and something to eat."

"Where did you go after that?" the Colonel enquired.

"When I left there, I just continued driving the way I had come, which led me to the Sentinel. I stopped to take a closer look. I'd never seen a tree like it before, ancient, commanding. It seemed to ooze both a sense of comfort and a forbidding sense of danger at the same time. I was fascinated by it. It seemed to call to me. Foolish as that seemed. I was lucky to find David there. The rest, as they say, is history."

She had been lost in thought, reliving the journey as she spoke. The colonel's next question snapped her back to reality.

"If David Reeves had not been there, what do you think you would have done?"

Freya shrugged.

"What could I have done? I would have had to get back in the car and find my way home."

Colonel Winguard reached for her hand.

"Yet he was there waiting for you because it was me who sent him, and I wouldn't have sent him if my son had not been killed in action. I would have been the one given to the Sentinel and my son would have been the one to inherit Sentinel Cottage. But that was not meant to be. The Fates had woven our lives together, bringing us to the same place and time to fulfil the destiny they had planned for us."

Freya could see the colonel's point. She had reached the same conclusion herself. But something he had said bothered her.

"What do you mean about your son being given to the Sentinel?"

Before the colonel could reply, the nurse entered the room again.

"I'm sorry, Colonel, but it's time for your medication now. I can't leave it any longer. Perhaps your visitor would like to have a coffee in the visitors' café and come back a little later?"

Freya took the hint, assuring the colonel that she would wait until he was ready to receive her again, but she was frustrated that her question had not been answered.

She was eating a sandwich when one of the care assistants arrived to tell her the colonel was resting and to ask her to make another appointment to see him.

"I'm so sorry for the inconvenience, but the colonel tires very easily these days. I'm sure you understand."

Freya did. His frailty had been clear to see. She made an appointment for the following day.

The colonel's body may have been frail, but his mind remained sharp, as Freya discovered when she visited him the following day. He was ready to pick up where they had left off.

"Ms Fraser, forgive my rudeness yesterday. You asked what I meant about my son being given to the Sentinel. Bear with me, for it is best explained with a brief history lesson. Would you like a cup of tea or coffee before we start?"

"That would be lovely. Thank you."

It was ordered with a simple press of a buzzer. It was delivered, along with biscuits, in no time and the Colonel began.

"Some of this I know you are familiar with. I have read the fine study your grandson has carried out, quite notable for one so young. You will know the history of the Sentinel goes much further back than the Norse occupation, but it is with the Norse that I must begin. The first Norseman to hold the land was Erik, as you know. But what you may not know is that Erik was the one who adopted the Sentinel, dedicating it to Heimdall, one of the Norse gods, as a symbol of protection. Do you know anything about Heimdall, Ms Fraser?"

Freya shook her head.

"Nothing, I'm afraid. But that explains why the land was known as Heimdall's land. Aston and I thought he was a past owner." Freya blushed with embarrassment at her ignorance.

"A natural assumption. The Norse belief system is a fascinating topic to explore. They believed in many gods, each with their own purpose and mythology. But let us stick with Heimdall. He is often called the 'Golden God', because he shone brighter than any of the other gods. He was also known as 'the Divine Sentinel'.

Freya gave a gasp, the mention of Heimdall as a sentinel, must surely be the connection with the ancient tree. She said nothing however, letting the colonel carry on.

"His home was Himinbjorg, in the land of the Vanir, but it was close to where the rainbow bridge, Bitfrost, met the sky, where the land of the Aesir, Asgard, could be found. His job was to keep watch for invaders and raise the alarm if any came, by blowing on the horn he carried for this purpose."

The colonel was giving her lots of information, which she knew she would never remember. As discreetly as she could, without disturbing the colonel's flow, Freya took a notebook and pen from her bag and began making notes as the colonel continued with his story,

"Crossing Bitfrost was the only way to reach Asgard. As an extra precaution, it was protected by fire. The belief was that should Asgard ever be breached, it would lead to Ragnarök, the battle that would be the end of the world."

Freya was becoming overwhelmed with information, all new to her, she found she had to interrupt the colonel in order to make things clearer in her head,

"Out of the many Gods, what made Heimdall stand out enough to be chosen for the task of look-out? she asked.

The colonel smiled,

"I'm just coming to that. Heimdall was Asgard's first line of defence, not only because his home was strategically positioned, but also because he was gifted with keen sight and keener hearing. It was said that he could hear a single leaf as it fell from the tree, even the sound of the growing grass. He was also gifted with foresight, so his senses would give plenty of warning of anyone approaching the bridge. He was the Watchman of the Gods."

As the colonel stopped to take a drink of water, Freya asked, "I can see why Heimdall was important to the other gods. But why did Erik choose to honour him above all the others?"

The colonel offered her a biscuit and rang for more tea, Astutely Freya realised this was a delaying tactic, allowing him to take a break. He was tiring. She fished in her bag, taking out photographs of Fen and Arty and handing them to the colonel.

"I almost forgot about these. I thought you might be interested to see them."

She drank her tea in companionable silence as the colonel shuffled through the images. When he appeared fixated on one particular image, she noticed that in fact he had fallen asleep. She walked quietly to the door and beckoned a carer to see to his needs.

"When he wakes, please tell him I'll be back tomorrow, all being well."

She made the appointment on the way out. Before she left, she asked the receptionist, "Is there anything the colonel needs? It occurs to me that he may not have many visitors. So, if he needs anything, or has a favourite treat, I'd be happy to bring anything to him."

The receptionist smiled.

"Bless you. I think he's doing well enough. There are two gentlemen who visit him regularly. I think they're from the army. They always bring him what he needs, and a little treat now and then. He has a fondness for ginger cake."

Freya thanked her and made a mental note to put ginger cake on her shopping list.

After completing her shopping in the new town, she drove to Marie's, arriving just as Aston came home from school. They met in the driveway, both giving each other a hug.

"Hi, Nan! I didn't know you were coming," was his opening remark.

"It's just a flying visit. I have some news for you. But let's go in and say hello to your mum first."

Marie was in the kitchen. Aston shouted to her, "I'm home, Mum, and Nan's here!" before running upstairs.

Freya made her way to the kitchen.

"Hi, Mum," said Marie, giving Freya a kiss. "To what do we owe this unexpected pleasure? Are you staying for tea?"

"No, thanks. It's just a flying visit. I've been visiting Colonel Winguard and I've picked up some news up for Aston."

"Colonel Winguard? He's the one who sold you Sentinel Cottage, isn't he?" Marie asked.

"He is. He wrote to me and asked me to visit him to discuss, as he put it, a matter beneficial to us both. But I've visited him twice now and I still don't know what it is. The poor man is very ill, and he rambles a bit. By the time he's given me the background of whatever is on his mind, he's too tired to get to the nitty gritty. I feel so guilty. I know I should have visited him sooner to thank him for the generous terms of the sale."

"Well, regrets won't change anything. Will you visit him again?"

"I'm going back tomorrow, if he's well enough to receive visitors. Even though he rambles, he's interesting to listen to. It's very sad to think all that knowledge he has will be lost when he dies. He talked about Norse religion today, and I picked up something interesting about Erik to pass on to Aston before I forget."

"What is it?" Aston asked. He had entered the room quietly while they were speaking, having changed out of his school uniform.

"You were right about the Sentinel pre-dating Norse occupation," Freya told him. "But Erik was the one who dedicated the tree to Heimdall, the Norse god. It was Heimdall's job to keep watch for invaders. He was known as the Divine Sentinel. That must be how the Sentinel got its name."

"That's cool! Did the colonel give you the source for his information?"

"Sadly not. I asked him what was special about Heimdall that made Erik choose him above all the other Norse gods, but he fell asleep before he could answer me. He really is very sick."

"That's sad. I'll look Heimdall up on Google, see what I can find, and if there is a source, we can use it to research further." Although his assignment was complete Aston was still eager to find out as much as he could.

"Brilliant! I'll leave it in your capable hands. Let me know what you find." Freya gave Aston the notes she had made before making her farewells, declining again the offer of tea. "Thank you, but no. I'll have to get back to Fen and Arty. I've been out most of the day. Speak to you soon."

Leaving Marie to finish cooking their meal, she let herself out.

It was two days before Freya was able to visit Colonel Winguard again. The nursing home telephoned to postpone and rearrange her appointment. Luckily, she wasn't left to wait too long to discover why Erik was likely to have a special regard for Heimdall. Aston had been as good as his word, sending her a message the same night. It seemed that Heimdall held a special place in the hearts of seafarers who relied on the keen senses attributed to him, but also because it was said that he had been birthed by nine goddesses who personified the sea. It was a natural choice, then, for Erik the Trader. Somehow, with her own roots in the seaside town of Whitby, this information brought Erik and the Sentinel even closer to Freya's heart.

The colonel was well rested and in fine form when Freya finally got to see him. His eyes lit up when she gave him the ginger cake. He handed it to the carer who had escorted Freya in.

"Can you cut a few slices and bring tea to go with it, Betsy? Thank you. Now, Ms Fraser, where did we leave off?"

"We were talking about Erik and the Sentinel, and why he had dedicated it to Heimdall," Freya reminded him.

"Ah, yes, I remember. Erik's tenure of the land was in a very turbulent period. There was much infighting among the Danes vying for the kingship of Northumbria. Kings came, went, and came again. Added to this, the Anglo-Saxon kings were determined to establish their own control over the region, to annexe it to England and unite the country under one rule and one king. For the most part, Jorvik itself carried on undisturbed, but for the outlying landowners, like Erik, there were new threats of eviction, new demands for taxes, where they had not been demanded before. The threat of violence was ever present. No wonder, then, that he chose to defend his land, just as the gods had chosen to defend Asgard, with Heimdall's help, as the Devine Sentinel, the watcher for any signs of trouble."

Betsy crept in with the tea and cake, and whispered, "Don't mind me. I'll just put these down and won't disturb you."

Freya took a sip of her tea and the colonel sampled the ginger cake before he continued.

"Erik defended the land for many years, living peacefully for most of them, until trouble came once more. He was growing old and close to death by this time. But still he protected the land as best he could. Ultimately, he sacrificed himself to secure Heimdall's continued protection."

Freya had not expected this. She gave an involuntary gasp.

"How?" she murmured

"He was already ill, confined to his bed from which he would never rise. He gave orders that he was to be carried to the Sentinel, and there to be bound, still breathing, to a branch of the tree and left to die, honouring Heimdall with his last breath and feeding the Sentinel with the last of his life's blood. This was the original act of sacrifice on the land from which all others derived. With Erik's death, the land and the role of protector went to his daughter, Freyja."

"I thought the land was meant to pass to Erik's son, Gorm" Freya queried.

"It should have passed to Gorm, but he had long since left on his own adventures. Legend has it that Freyja had been chosen by the Seidr to establish a dynasty of protectors, who would give their last breath to protect the land and the Sentinel for all time. She fulfilled that prediction, eventually following the same path of sacrifice that her father had chosen. And so it went on, unbroken, from protector to protector. In time, living sacrifice was replaced by binding the earthly body of the protector to the tree, as a burial practice, the intent being that the corpse would feed and nourish the tree, keeping it strong and healthy. Eventually it was the cremated remains that were offered, as it was with my son. As it will be for me, with your consent."

Freya was shocked beyond words. This was something she had not foreseen. After doing everything she could to protect the Sentinel by keeping people away from it, her instinct was to refuse, but she also believed that it was a basic human right for a person to be buried according to their own customs. She was dealing with an established custom and the request of a dying man, the last of his line. How could she deny him his right?

She bought herself more time to consider her decision.

"My grandson communicates with Erik. Before we knew who he was, he called him 'the man who lives in the tree'. He has also mentioned several times that Fen and Arty belong 'to the man in the tree'. I know they don't belong to Erik, but in light of what you have just told me, is my grandson also seeing your son?"

The colonel gave Freya an assessing stare before replying.

"The spirits are strong, and your grandson has more gifts than I thought. Yes, my son will be close by. But your grandson is in no danger from the spirits of the land. They know change is coming. They will gather to welcome me into their midst, and to transfer their loyalty to you and yours."

"Me! What have I got to do with it? I own the land thanks to you, but I can't trace my ancestry beyond my great-grandparents. Certainly not to Freyja."

The colonel shrugged.

"That may be true, but the connection is there. The name 'Fraser' is it your maiden name?

Freya nodded, somewhat perplexed how the colonel could have known she had stopped using her married name many years ago. The colonel did not acknowledge her response and carried on speaking

"The name Fraser has been corrupted over time from Freyja's. By the time she married and had children she had become a powerful seidr, feared and respected in her community. She did not take her husband's name, and it was her name that was passed on to her children who would have been Freyjason or Freyjasdottir. The Sentinel recognised you and called you to be where you are today."

"Forgive me, Colonel, but how can you be sure?"

"I had to be certain I was passing the land on to the right person. The end of my life is approaching, and I have no heir, but that didn't mean that Freyja had no heir. She had many children and grandchildren, who in turn carried her genes down through time. Just like my own line. I asked for guidance and was told the heir would answer the call of the Sentinel's spirits, and would pass three tests, or signs. The first, of course, was answering the call, as you did, subconsciously. The second was that the heir would show a natural desire to protect the Sentinel. You warned David Reeves of the danger the tree faced from developers destroying the land, and unbidden, you have taken steps to safeguard it from such a fate. The third test asked for the heir to undertake a personal trial, in order to show their worthiness to be handed the responsibility to protect the

173

Sentinel and the land. I set that trial by requiring you to adopt and care for Fen and Arty. You went further than I expected by dedicating yourself to the training that was required of you, and you have accomplished more than I expected in so short a time. You, Freya Freyjasdottir, are the rightful heir."

The threads linking all this together were intricate, but Freya recognised that they added up to far more than chance. Her throat was dry.

"Could I have a cup of tea, please?" she managed to ask.

"Of course. Forgive me. I have overloaded you with information. But I am almost done, if you will bear with me a little while longer. Better to deal with it now than leave things unsaid."

The tea arrived and Freya took several grateful sips, before asking,

"What do I have to do?"

"For the most part, carry on as you have been. But there are certain requirements and restrictions you will have to agree to, though these are not in my remit to discuss at this point and will most likely fall to another who will explain it all."

"What about the scattering of your ashes? How does that work? Is there a ceremony or rite that needs to be followed?"

The colonel visibly relaxed, breathing out a silent sigh as though he recognised that, with this question, Freya had given her consent to his request.

"Offering one's earthly remains to the Sentinel and Heimdall is the last official duty of the outgoing protector, and facilitating that offering is the first official duty of the incoming protector. I will leave my instructions. There is an organisation, known as the Warriors of Freyja, whose duty it is to support you in your responsibilities. You will find no mention of them in any written source but know that you will not be alone. For the protection of the organisation, keep what I have shared with you to yourself. In your new role, a degree of secrecy and discretion is required."

He rang the bell and Betsy came in, carrying a box. It was obviously prearranged, for when she handed it to the colonel, she whispered,

"I hope you've managed to get everything sorted now, Colonel."

"Thank you, Betsy, I have. Ms Fraser has been very patient with me."

As Betsy departed, the colonel handed the box to Freya.

"This is for your eyes only. The contents will aid you in your future duties. Now, you have given me your time most generously, and my thanks go with you most sincerely, Ms Fraser."

As Freya reached the door, the colonel called to her again.

"Thank you for your kindness and generosity. Now I know all will be as it should be, I can let myself rest. I no longer have any need to fight the inevitable. Goodbye, Ms Fraser."

"Goodbye, Colonel."

28

Following the Path

Freya left with sadness in her heart, knowing she would not see the colonel again in this life. At home, after parking the car in the driveway, she walked across to stand before the Sentinel.

"Am I doing the right thing?" she whispered.

Though autumn was well established, the Sentinel was still fully dressed in its summer glory of green leaves. Freya watched as, seemingly in response to her question, the great tree shed its cloak as a wind rose from nowhere and every leaf fell to the ground instantly. A voice, real or only in her mind, echoed,

"The way will be open."

As she looked upon the naked Sentinel for the first time, she noticed the ancient oak bore a cavity within its huge trunk. The opening looked like an arched doorway with nothing but deep darkness beyond. She stared into the depths for a long time, unsure whether she could see movement within the blackness. Suddenly feeling uncomfortable, she stepped back.

"Thank you for your guidance," she murmured, before retreating to the safety of her cottage. Now feeling emotionally drained, she felt in need of a complete rest from all things Norse for the time being.

It was very close to Halloween, which normally took most of her attention as it was traditionally a family time, full of fun and laughter. But their new life had opened doors to new traditions. Aston was intending to go trick or treating with his school friends, with Marie joining the other mums in escorting the children around the town. Rose was partying in York with her new friends, while Daniel's continued silent animosity would keep him out of the picture altogether. A short break was out of the question. After all, she could hardly book two wolves into an unsuspecting dog hotel. So there was only one other option.

She drove into Harrogate and caught the train to Leeds. She spent the day shopping, stockpiling the most simplistic of popular romances that would require no mind activity at all to read, plus a good selection of horror fiction. Added to this, a fresh selection of wine, chocolates and tasty snacks set her up for the night itself. She felt truly self-indulgent, never having had the time to relax and read before, or the funds to spare. She suddenly realised, as she was unpacking her goodies, that far from feeling abandoned on this, the first Halloween she would spend alone, she felt liberated. This was her time!

When the morning of Halloween arrived, Freya found she had few preparations to make (she reckoned her cottage was too isolated to attract trick or treaters), so she spent the day indulging the Fen and Arty and putting them through their paces. Even though it had been some weeks since she practised their training, they performed perfectly, showing their willingness to respond to her commands. For late October, the weather was bright and sunny, with no chilling wind to steal the warmth of the sun away. Freya enjoyed their extra-long walk, revelling in the peace and companionship of the wolves. She had grown to love them and knew they had given her their trust. By the end of the afternoon, she had even lost sight of it being Halloween, so different and relaxing had her day been.

Later, in the evening, she sat beside the glowing fire, a glass of ginger wine and a box of chocolates beside her as she read one of her chosen books. It was an old Stephen King, *Salem's Lot*, perfect for Halloween. She was beginning to doze off when the haunting howl of the wolves pierced the air. Instantly, she was not only awake but moving quickly to the garage, to check on the animals.

The first thing she noticed as she flicked on the light was that the garage door and the garden door remained firmly locked from the inside. The second was the wolves. They both stood on their hind legs, pressed close to the mesh of the pen, their feet dancing and tails wagging. They were excited, not alarmed.

A kneeling figure beside the pen stood up, giving the wolves a final scratch of their ears through the mesh.

"At rest now, privates."

As he spoke, both wolves immediately lay back down.

Freya had already recognised the intruder, if he could indeed be described as such, wearing his military uniform and with the same dazzling smile she had seen in his photograph, it was undoubtedly Major Winguard, the colonel's son and former handler of the wolves. In her mind she questioned how this could be. He was dead, wasn't he?

He turned to her, giving her a salute.

"It is time to return my father to where he belongs, Protector. Follow the marked path and you will be guided in all things."

Before she could respond, the major had vanished, leaving only Freya and the now-sleeping wolves in the room. Instinctively she checked the external doors again. Both remained locked from the inside. She made her way quickly back to the living room to look out of the bay window at the Sentinel. It was lit by an ethereal golden glow. She could see flames flickering around its trunk.

"Oh, sweet lord! It's on fire!" she cried in panic. "The Sentinel is on fire!"

She rushed unthinking to the front door, flinging it wide open. Then she stopped in her tracks.

From her front door all the way to the Sentinel, cloaked and hooded figures made a double-lined pathway to the great tree. Each carried a burning torch to light the way. She could see now that the flames she had thought were issuing from the Sentinel were more of these flaming torches, held by the continuing line of hooded figures who eventually encircled the tree. The bright golden light enshrouding the Sentinel even eclipsed the glorious full moon, making its silver glow insignificant.

From the depths of the flames, a clear voice, not loud, but capturing an echo, called out.

"Freya Freyjasdottir! It is time to make your offering. Return our brother, with honour, to his rightful place among his ancestors, and make your pledge to follow his path."

Though the colonel had done his best to prepare her for this moment, it was with a pounding heart that Freya stepped forward, following the path marked out by the hooded figures. As she passed, they fell in behind her, until she led a torch-lit procession that came to a halt at the base of the Sentinel. The way forward was now barred by the imposing presence of a woman. A plain blue dress was visible beneath a dark cloak, held together by a circular brooch of plaited silver, which bore at its centre the rune Fehu, the symbol for beginnings and endings. Freya recognised the rune from notes she had found in the box of papers given to her by the Colonel. The woman's grey hair was bound into a complex coil of braids and her face was lined with age, though her piercing blue eyes danced with life and an all-knowing intelligence.

She took a step towards Freya.

"Be welcome, Freya Freyjasdottir. Give me your hand."

Freya did as she was bid. The woman held her hand gently, palm up, caressing it with her thumb, before looking up. She held Freya's eyes with her own.

"You know who I am. Name me and give me recognition," she commanded.

"I believe you to be Freyja Eriksdottir," Freya replied. "I give you greeting and honour for all you overcame and for all that you achieved. For all that you continue to achieve."

The woman nodded slowly and thoughtfully.

"You recognise me with your heart, but your mind is doubtful. You doubt your own lineage, do you not? Do you think that I, given the gifts of the Seidr who gave me back my life and prophesied my life's purpose, would not recognise my own blood kin? Would the mighty god Heimdall make a mistake in predicting your coming? The Norns set your path, as they set mine, to bring us together at this place, on this night, for this purpose. Cast aside your doubts, Freya Freyjasdottir, and give your ancestors recognition."

Freya looked about her, seeing, beyond the ring of black-clad figures, the faces of hundreds, if not thousands, of men, women and children, who packed the land on which the Sentinel had stood for centuries. Their attire, where it was visible, represented every period of English history right up to the present day. Major Winguard stood very close by.

Awestruck, Freya hesitated only a moment longer as she processed the enormity of Freyja's legacy. Then she felt a gentle squeeze of her fingers.

She knelt.

"I give thanks and honour to Freyja Eriksdottir, to her father Erik, and to each and every one of you, my ancestors, for your care and protection of this land. For your lifetime of dedication and the lives given freely in carrying out your sworn duty. Because of you, I am now privileged to call this my home. I freely dedicate my life to follow in your footsteps, and I pledge that I will nurture and protect this land for all time. Hail, Freyja Eriksdottir! Hail Heimdall!"

She had no idea why she had spoken the last five words, but they proved popular, as the dead and the living shouted in unison, "Hail, Freyja Eriksdottir! Hail Heimdall!" And they repeated the cry several times.

Freya was helped to rise from her kneeling position, as Freyja addressed her for the last time that evening.

"You have made your pledge of your own free will and bound your fate with those who preceded you and those who will follow you. Your chosen path will have its difficulties, but you will never be alone. My living warriors will now make their pledge to you. From this point on, they will be your guides, advisers, protectors and thralls."

As Freyja stepped back, two of the cloaked figures came forward. Hoods still firmly in place, they stood before Freya. Acting as one, the one on her right extended his left arm towards his companions on his left, while the one on her left did likewise to his companions on his right. The entire cloaked company knelt and, as one, made their pledge to Freya, as the Protector of the Sentinel. With their pledge made, the two leading warriors moved to either side of her. One handed her a finely carved box, which she was informed held the colonel's ashes. With no one now in front, Freya could see the dark mouth of the Sentinel begin to glow. An unidentified voice from somewhere unseen, gave her the first task she would perform as Protector of the Sentinel.

"Prepare to return our brother to our midst. Scatter his ashes among the roots of the Sentinel, symbolic of returning him to the roots of his ancestors."

Flanked by her anonymous escorts, Freya made her way carefully around the gnarled, snaking roots of the Sentinel, reaching intermittently into the box and scattering the colonel's ashes as she went. She felt the need to say something as she did so, something she felt would respect and honour the service given by the colonel. So, with each scattering, she murmured,

"I return you with honour to the roots of your ancestors."

She was surprised to hear her words repeated reverently by those close enough to hear. When, in due course, she found herself back at the glowing mouth of the tree, the empty box she now carried was replaced by a second box, carved with runes. The voice she heard seemed to come from within the Sentinel itself.

"You may now enter the heart of our world to return our loyal servant's heart to where it belongs."

Freya felt a moment of panic. What was she supposed to do? Just leave the box in the hollow of the tree, or bury it?

One of her companions bent down and whispered to her, "Don't worry. We will do what is necessary. You just have to carry the box to its resting place and oversee all is done well. Come."

Carrying, with reverence, the box containing the colonel's heart, Freya stepped into the cavity of the Sentinel alongside her companions. Above her head darkness swallowed the light from the flaming torches, while the ethereal golden glow dazzled her eyesight, like looking into the sun, it blinded her vision. They knelt. The floor was firm from compacted earth but rough shards, of dead wood (or bone) dug into her knees. Freya held the box protectively to her chest as the two warriors used their hands to make a shallow bowl in the floor of the tree. When they indicated they were happy with its depth, Freya handed over the box. She watched as the colonel's heart was removed from the box and placed into the scooped out hollow. For a moment, the golden glow brightened to a dazzling intensity before they were plunged into deepest darkness. An unnatural silence enfolded her. For what seemed an age, she remained kneeling, waiting for something to happen, perhaps some whispered word of instruction from the warriors. But nothing broke the silence. She was alone in the dark, inside the Sentinel.

It would have been easy to be engulfed by panic, but she fought it off.

"Think!" she said to herself. She had been sitting with her back to the opening. It should be easy to find, if she remained calm.

She spun on her hands and knees until she faced where the opening should be and crawled forward, feeling her way with her hands. The distance seemed interminable until at last she felt the solid wall of the cavity before her. She stood. She knew the opening was taller than she was. It must be close by. She would find it by following the solidity of the inner trunk. The only question was, would it be closer to her left or to her right?

She glanced around her. There was no sign of any light from outside filtering in, not even the moonlight. She decided to move to the right. Walking as though on a precipice, she felt her way with her hands before taking one step at a time sidewards.

Time passed. Her breath rasped, sweat dripped from her brow. She felt she had already covered the full circumference of the cavity. Had she misjudged the height of the opening and missed it? But no. She would surely have felt a draught of air from outside or seen a glimmer of moonlight.

She pressed on. Then it was there, just an arm's length away. Two more steps, then her arms were grabbed, and she was pulled through into light and air. Somebody placed a blanket around her shoulders.

"You all bear witness." Freyja's voice. "It has been done and done well. The old Protector has kept his vow unto death, his last act to feed his heart to the Sentinel. A new Protector now serves us. Heimdall has tested her and found her worthy of new birth. All hail to the Protector."

The words stirred the crowd, who joined in Freyja's call, until it reached a crescendo.

Once more Freya found herself flanked by two warriors. She had no idea if they were the same ones who had deserted her inside the tree, but they led her forward, retracing her steps to Sentinel Cottage. This time none of the warriors who lined her path fell in behind her, but each one extinguished their torch as she passed. By the time she reached Sentinel Cottage, the torches and her escort had faded into the ether. She stood alone in her own garden, the Sentinel and all around it stood bathed in darkness, save for the silvery light of the full moon.

For a minute or two Freya stood bewildered, unsure if what she experienced had been real or imaginary. How could it be real? Why would she imagine something so outside her own experience, something so bizarre? She looked at the dark shape of The Sentinel, lit by the silvery light of the full moon, the Hunters Moon it was called. She pulled the blanket tighter around her as she spoke to the ancient tree,

"You are far older and wiser than I. Your truths and traditions go far beyond my limited experience. I put my trust in you as you put your trust in me. Blessings and honour be yours on this night and always."

Safely inside her cottage once more, Freya noticed two things (after she had poured herself a stiff drink). Firstly, what she had assumed was a blanket was in fact Freyja's cloak, and secondly, beneath the cloak she was filthy. Her clothes, hands and face were begrimed by crawling around on the floor inside the Sentinel. Taking her brandy with her, she went for a bath, letting the hot, sweet-smelling water bathe and sooth her, fighting the need to analyse the events of the evening. For now, she just wanted to revel in being clean, calm and secure in her own home.

Eventually, dressed in a sweatshirt and joggers, she took up her seat beside the fire, picking up where she had left off with her book. But the fact was she couldn't settle. The events of the evening were too disturbing. She was drawn constantly to the window, worried in case the Sentinel truly caught fire from a discarded torch. But all was well outside. Soon, though, she gave up any pretence of reading, thinking she would walk off her restlessness by taking Fen and Arty out.

The thought had barely formed when a loud knocking on the front door, accompanied by giggles and shouts of "trick or treat" through the letterbox, had her rushing to let in her unexpected visitors. She had recognised Aston's voice immediately. She opened the door so quickly he almost fell inside.

"It will have to be a trick, I'm afraid, I've eaten all the chocolates" she declared by way of greeting, ushering Aston and his mum in as she spoke, delighted with their visit.

"Don't worry," said Marie, dressed as the Bride of Dracula. "We've brought loads of goodies. We both missed being with you so much we couldn't stay away." She hugged her mother, adding, "What have you been doing?"

Freya shrugged.

"Oh, nothing to write home about. I'm so pleased you came."

Freya felt guilty keeping her secret from Aston. But she told herself that one day she would tell him, just not for many years to come. It was not yet his time.

Freya was both a pragmatist and an optimist, no matter what life threw at her she always held on to the thought that things would work out in the end. Although she had heard nothing from Daniel for some time, she believed that the day would come when they were reconciled. For the present it was enough for them all to be together, making new memories and new traditions in Sentinel Cottage.

Epilogue

Many years would pass before Freya had to make her own arrangements for her final commitment to the Sentinel and pass on to her successor those secrets needed to be a responsible Protector of the Sentinel and the settlement. In the intermediate years, they would have many joint adventures and discover more hidden secrets as they continued to uncover the history of the land and the Norse settlement they cared for. Maybe one day, I will share their ongoing story with you …

Historical Figures Mentioned in the Text

St Olave (Olaf II, King of Norway) 1015–28
King Aethelred the Unready 978–1013
King Cnut 900–5
Jarl Siward of Northumbria 1041–55
King Olaf Guthfrithson of Northumbria 939–41
King Olafr Sigtryggson of Northumbria 941–3/4
Eric Bloodaxe of Northumbria 947–9/952–4

Norse Gods and Goddesses

Heimdall
Freyja
Thor
Njord
Odin
Hel

Mystical Beings of the Norse Belief System

The Husvaettir – house sprites/spirits, mostly benign, but their
favour needed to be cultivated by showing them honour or
they could become mischievous
The Nisse and Illvatte – mischievous/hostile spirits/sprites
The Norns – three sisters who sit at the foot of Yggdrasil weaving
and spinning the fates of all on earth
Valkyries – female spirits in the service of the god Odin and
goddess Freyja to transport the souls of the heroic dead to
Valhalla or Sessrumnir